W9-AVK-206

3 1526 04328363 6

The 13th Sign

Kristin O'Donnell Tubb

WITHDRAWN

FEIWEL AND FRIENDS

NEW YORK

A FEIWEL AND FRIENDS BOOK
An Imprint of Macmillan

THE 13TH SIGN. Copyright © 2013 by Kristin O'Donnell Tubb. All rights reserved.
Printed in the United States of America by R. R. Donnelley & Sons Company,
Harrisonburg, Virginia. For information, address Feiwel and Friends, 175 Fifth
Avenue, New York, N.Y. 10010.

Library of Congress Cataloging-in-Publication Data

Tubb, Kristin O'Donnell.
The 13th sign / Kristin O'Donnell Tubb. — 1st ed.
p. cm.
Summary: On her thirteenth birthday, Jalen unwittingly brings the twelve signs of
the zodiac to life through a mysterious old book, and soon she, her friend Ellie, and
Ellie's brother, Brennan, are battling in the streets of New Orleans to defeat the
twelve and their little-known companion before time runs out.

ISBN: 978-0-312-58352-1 (hardcover) / 978-1-250-03766-4 (e-book)

[1. Supernatural—Fiction. 2. Zodiac—Fiction. 3. Astrology—Fiction.
4. Adventure and adventurers—Fiction. 5. Books and reading—Fiction.
6. New Orleans (La.)—Fiction.] I. Title. II. Title: Thirteenth sign.
PZ7.T796Aah 2013
[Fic]—dc23
2012034058

Book design by Ashley Halsey

Feiwel and Friends logo designed by Filomena Tuosto

First Edition: 2013

10 9 8 7 6 5 4 3 2 1

mackids.com

For two Pisces and a Gemini
(or a Pisces, an Aquarius, and a Taurus?)

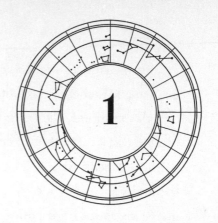

S agittarius: Your bubbly personality and effervescent style make you a shoo-in for 'Most Likely to Be the Center of Attention at a Party. Straighten that tiara, flash those pearly whites, and dance for your admirers, superstar!' "

Madame Beausoleil finished reading my horoscope from the ancient book in her lap. She raised her gaze to mine. Madame's eyes were foggy with age, though she claimed her cloudy eyes helped her to "see." I didn't know Madame well myself; I usually came here with my Nina. Madame called herself a voodoo priestess, and her milky eyes, her whole dark and dusty shop, gave me the chills. Armies of carved wooden masks stared from the walls with empty eye sockets. Dream catchers and incense burners and wind chimes hung from the ceiling like swarms of ghosts jangling their chains. Visitors were warned with scratchy, hand-printed signs: "ABSOLUTELY *NO* PHOTOS."

But I had to overlook the creepiness. Coming to Beausoleil/Fâchénuit (Beautiful Sun/Angry Night) was my birthday tradition. *Our* birthday tradition—mine and Nina's. I had to come, even if Nina couldn't. Used to be—once upon a time—Daddy would come with us, too. He'd dig through the junky shelves, wide-eyed, for hours, asking thousands of questions about horoscopes and zodiacs and such. Madame Beausoleil would eventually get so fed up with him she'd kick him out, shooing him away and telling him to never come back. And Nina would laugh and say, "See you next birthday!"

I shook that thought off with a pang. "Honestly?" I asked now. "That's what my horoscope says? I don't even own a tiara." Ellie spat a laugh at my side. The salt-and-pepper snake in the glass box on the counter knotted into a tighter coil.

My horoscope always read like that, and it could not be more wrong. I didn't act, think, feel, dance, dress, play, work, or love like a Sagittarian. I'd hoped a reading from Madame Beausoleil might be more accurate.

Maybe I had misunderstood. Madame Beausoleil spoke with a thick Creole accent, like her mouth was full of spicy peppers. So I asked again, "Is that really what it says about me?"

I looked to Ellie, who stood next to an overstuffed display of voodoo dolls, pins launching forth from their rag-doll

bodies like shooting stars, their instruments of torture en-
tangling them in a voodoo universe. Ellie placed a hand over
her mouth to stifle a giggle, but she was definitely smiling.
Even Madame Beausoleil's eyes twinkled with amusement at
how inaccurate this picture of me was.

"Dat's what it say, girl." Madame's leather-brown skin
pulled taut, showing her huge gap-toothed grin. "You don'
tink *Seventeen* magazine got you pegged?" She reached between the pages of the huge tome on her lap, pulled out a
tattered magazine, and tossed it toward me. There, on the
cover, between gleaming-white movie star smiles, scrawled
in neon green font: "Happy Birthday, Sagittarius!!! Read inside to see what the upcoming year holds for Y-O-U, superstar!!!"

I wanted to scream and shout at being duped like this.
I wanted to demand my money back. Instead, I twiddled
my fingers in the hot-pink streak dyed in my hair, pulling the lock across my face. I managed only to whisper in
a shaky voice, "You said you'd give me a *real* horoscope
reading."

But Madame had already moved on to picking the dirt
from beneath her fingernails with a huge knife blade attached to an ivory handle. "Why should I?" she asked. "Girl
don' believe dis hoo anyways, now do she? Every year she
come here, every year she scoff. Now, go shop." She didn't
look up from her fingernail cleaning, just jerked her head at

the rest of the store behind us. Her multicolored turban bobbed as she did.

I sighed. No, I *didn't* believe this hoo. It seemed unlikely that my personality could be controlled by my zodiac sign, that my birthdate and a bunch of stars could define me. Horoscopes were nothing but words on paper. How could that possibly shape the future? No, it seemed much more likely that we humans were messing up all on our own.

But my Nina *did* believe in this hoo—just as my dad had—and she brought me to Beausoleil/Fâchénuit every year on my birthday to have my tea leaves read, or my palm studied, or my tarot cards flipped. But this year, on my thirteenth birthday, Nina wasn't with me. Breast cancer had my Nina trapped in a spiderweb of tubes and needles. And I wasn't even allowed in the hospital room. My mom was by her side, but Mom hardened whenever tragedy clawed its way into our home. Which was far too often.

Ellie checked the clock on her cell phone. "We'd better hurry, Jalen. Brennan will be ticked if he has to park the car and come inside."

As if on cue, Brennan entered the tiny dark store, chiming the bells tied to the door. He ducked beneath a row of alligator teeth on a string. The image of Brennan getting swallowed whole made me grin.

"Aren't y'all ready yet?" he grumbled. "It's been five

minutes!" Ellie shot him a wide-eyed look, but Brennan scowled back. "Look, Ellie. Don't start with the sick-grandma stuff. I don't want to hear it. And I'm not waiting long."

I rolled my eyes and cursed breast cancer once again. With Nina sick, Ellie and I had been forced to bum a ride with her brother Brennan. He was only fifteen, but he'd been driving a massive, rusting pickup truck around the streets of New Orleans since he was thirteen. Ellie and Brennan's parents were quite lax about things like, oh, the law.

"Patience, Brennan," I cooed at him, knowing it'd drive him nuts. I reached into one of the hundreds of nearby jars. "Here. Suck on a peppermint-soaked bamboo stick. It's supposed to calm you." Under my breath—*way* under, so no one could hear—I added, "And shut you up." I *wanted* to say stuff like that out loud, but I figured it wasn't worth the trouble.

Brennan glared at me and looked like he was about to say something else, but Ellie stepped between us. I was glad she did; I wasn't up for his teasing tonight. He spun and headed for the display of ceremonial drums. He smiled at one and tapped on it a bit—*tap tap tippetty tap*—but he stopped when he saw me watching him. He scowled and moved on to the glimmering crystal collection. I got a little teary at that. Crystals were Nina's favorite.

Ellie must've sensed my already sour mood taking a nose-dive, because she steered me to the other side of the store.

"Let's look at the books," she said. Ellie always knew how to cheer me up.

I looked at some of the titles of the books and couldn't help but smirk at their spines. *Your Many Past Lives* and *You Can: Realign your Chakras!* and *Healing through Meditation*. Yes, if only it were that easy. I sighed and pulled that title off the shelf, just to see if maybe Mom and I were missing something. Anything to heal my Nina, to pull her a little farther away from the edge of death.

Behind that title, stuffed behind the other books, was a small brown leather book, hidden by the dusty collection in front of it. This book was crisscrossed with a metal chain, binding it both horizontally and vertically. Shut tight with a tiny brass lock.

I reached for it, this book tucked behind the others, hiding in the dark. It shocked me when I touched it. I jerked my finger back, and my ears popped with a whoosh.

Dusty metal, I thought. Madame Beausoleil really needs to clean this place.

Around the chain, I read the title, branded into the leather cover in a scrolly, burnt script: *The Keypers of the Zodiack*.

A book about horoscopes! Maybe this could give me a *real* view of my future, not some pop-vomit version from a magazine.

Ellie looked over my shoulder, and I felt her nod. "That's what we're getting."

We took the book to the counter. "Madame, um, Beau-soleil?" I asked. Addressing this woman directly made my heart race. "Where's the key to this book?"

Madame looked up, and the clouds in her eyes turned thunderous. "Dat's not fo sale. Where you find dat?"

"On the bookshelf," Ellie cut in. "There's a price tag on it. Thirty dollars."

"Not fo sale," she said, waggling her fingers at us in a give-it-here motion. "You not ready."

Not ready? Why does no one think a thirteen-year-old is ready? Not the hospital, not my mom, not this con artist voodoo priestess. But I gave the book to her. Her hands felt like cool paper.

Madame tucked the book under the counter. "Keep look-ing, girls," she said. She stood and shuffled through a thick purple curtain into a back room. The snake in the glass box on the counter lifted its head and blinked a single black eye. Winked?

"Yeah, and make it quick," Brennan said over his shoul-der. He'd moved on to the other rock displays and was palming a smooth geode, the kind of rock that was plain Jane on the outside, but you shattered it with the hope there would be spectacular crystals inside. It's likely the only thing that gets better *after* being shattered.

Ellie hopped up on the counter, leaned over, snagged the book. After she grabbed it, she looked at the cover for a moment, like it might've shocked her, too. She shrugged and tossed $40 on the counter.

"Let's go," she whispered.

"Ellie!" I snapped. My eyes darted to the curtain. Madame Beausoleil could likely *feel* what we were doing in here.

"What?" Ellie asked. "That crazy lady is asking for this. She ripped you off, making you pay for a horoscope reading from *Seventeen* magazine. And she calls herself a friend of your Nina."

Ellie punched all the right buttons. *She's right,* I thought. And it wasn't like we were stealing the book. In fact, we were overpaying.

"Let's go," I whispered back. I tucked the book into the front of my jeans. The chain scratched my stomach, and a little bead of blood appeared.

Brennan, Ellie, and I scooted out of Beausoleil/Fâchénuit and into the dark, cool night. The streets of New Orleans's French Quarter were eerily bare. Rain from earlier in the day glimmered under the streetlamps on the brick-inlaid sidewalks and made them look like they were made of nighttime sky, dark and light contrasted.

Like she were reading my mind, Ellie said, "Jalen, it's your birthday. Wish on a star." I glanced her way, but Ellie's face was upturned, not looking down like mine.

I shrugged. I felt very uncomfortable about this book. Not

uncomfortable about it crammed in my jeans and scratching me, although, *yes*, that was awkward. Uncomfortable about taking something I'd been told I shouldn't have. I realized my fingers were tangled in a pink streak of hair.

"Nah," I said. "No use. I have more wishes than stars."

2

Leaning against the passenger side window of Brennan's pickup, I tugged and pulled at the chain binding *The Keypers of the Zodiack*. It was no use; the chain would not budge, and I didn't want to damage the book. I examined the lock: brass, very intricate. The lock itself was shaped like a heart, with two snakes twined together around it. The scaly snakes looped above the heart, bodies coiling, forming the handle of the lock. Their eyes, narrowed at each another in strike mode, were emerald-green jewels. Their tongues, quick and wispy. The whole thing would make a really incredible tattoo—maybe someday. Something about the lock—the snakes, the heart—seemed eerily familiar to me. Déjà vu. I shivered.

"Is this the right way?" Ellie bent down and peered under the rearview mirror, looking up at the passing street sign. As if *her* navigation skills would get us home. Ellie was many wonderful things, but a reliable navigator? No.

Brennan half smiled. "Ellie. You always know where you are in New Orleans—"

"—if you just know were the river is." All three of us repeated this. It was Brennan's driving mantra. It was true, though. I loved that about New Orleans. The river was a comforting compass.

"Just don't forget to take the bridge, Brennan. No ferries."

Brennan huffed, and my face grew hot. They were avoiding the ferry because of me, because of my fear of boats. I hated that. But I wasn't about to ride that ferry.

Ellie's phone rang, some cheesy folk song blasting from her pocket. Brennan snorted. She looked at the screen, then passed the phone to me. "It's the drill sergeant."

My mom. I wished Ellie wouldn't use that nickname for her in front of Brennan. My mom called me on Ellie's phone all the time. It was her way of working around getting me a phone of my own.

"Hello?" I whispered.

"I hadn't heard from you yet. Are you home?" I could hear the click of my mom's heels echoing in the tile halls of the hospital.

"Mom, it's 8:03."

"Are you home?"

I sighed. "Almost."

I could practically hear my mom's shoulders drop a notch or two. "Good. Did you have fun?"

"Yeah." I wanted so badly to add, *"I wish Nina could've come,"* but I didn't dare say something like that in the cab of Brennan's truck.

Mom paused, like she knew what I wanted to say. "Want to talk to her?"

"Sure."

Heels clicked, the phone shuffled, and then that Southern accent slow as honey poured through Ellie's phone. "Jalen," Nina's voice sang.

I smiled.

"Jalen, love, thank heavens you went to Beausoleil/ Fâchénuit without me! Did you get your horoscope read?"

"Yes, ma'am."

"Well, thank heavens. Can't catch your dreams if you don't know what the path ahead looks like. What a brave girl you are to go to that scary voodoo shop all by your lonesome."

I giggled and so did Nina. She loved that scary voodoo shop.

Nina coughed, and it was like an alarm, reminding me where she was. "You feeling okay?" I asked.

"Sure, love. Sure. Hospital food tastes just like birthday cake, don't you know?"

We said our good-byes, and Mom made me promise to call every hour until we went to sleep. I passed the phone back to Ellie. *"Thank heavens,"* Nina's voice sang in my head. *"Can't catch your dreams if you don't know what the path ahead looks like."* If only she knew what a con artist her friend Madame Beausoleil was. According to her, my path ahead required a tiara.

Brennan approached my house. I was always a little embarrassed about the outside of my home—the peeling paint, the sagging gutters—and anytime I saw it through someone else's eyes, I felt defensive. And inside? Our furniture was old and dusty, our high-ceiling corners filled with cobwebs. Deteriorating, like everything eventually did. It was hard, me and Mom and Nina keeping up an old house like ours. When Daddy was here, this place had been a showstopper. Now it was just filled with ghosts and memories. Which are really the same thing, when you think about it.

"This is fine." I bolted upright and leaned across Ellie to speak to Brennan. He huffed and slammed to a stop at the corner of my yard. He'd had that temper since we were kids. I used to find it amusing. Now I found it annoying.

Ellie plucked the book off my lap. "Maybe I could pick the lock. You know, all spy-like?" She jimmied the keyhole with her electric-green pinkie fingernail. We hopped out of Brennan's truck, and he peeled away, wheels squealing. Show-off.

Ellie handed me *The Keypers of the Zodiack,* and we went inside, straight to the pottery wheel. Mom had converted an old sunroom on the side of our house into a small pottery studio. Throwing pots is messy business, and this sunroom was constantly covered in a film of mud.

"These tools." I pointed to a row of picks and brushes used to make designs in the clay. "Let's try them." But after a good ten minutes of unsuccessfully trying to pick the lock, I gave up.

I tossed the book on a rickety wicker chair, picked up a hunk of clay covered in plastic wrap, opened it, and pounded it. I prepared my slip and turned the wheel on. When my foot pressed the pedal, spatters of gray muck fanned everywhere.

"Hey!" Ellie hopped backward. "You did that on purpose!" She laughed, swiping at the drops of mud on her peace-sign sweatshirt.

I smiled. "You know not to stand that close."

My hands sank into the cool, slick mud, and I felt all my anger at Madame Beausoleil, at Brennan, at cancer ooze between my fingers and spin into that pot. I centered the clay first, sculpting a small tower in the middle of the wheel, on the spinning wooden bat. Once the column was right, I pushed my thumbs into the top. The lump of clay rounded, then hollowed out, turning from something useless into something practical. Spinning chaos into order.

All my pots look the same. Some are a little taller, some a little wider, but they're all basically bowls. Every once in a while my mom tries to get me to try a new shape, like a vase or something. When she does, I end up pressing the spinning wheel too hard with my foot, pinching the clay too thin with my fingers, and then I lose the bowl altogether.

"Bolt cutters," Ellie was saying when I turned the wheel off. She flicked the snake lock on *The Keypers of the Zodiack*.

"What's that?" I took the bat off the wheel. I put it and the bowl on the drying rack next to a half dozen other pots.

"You never fire them," Ellie said, looking up from the book at the filled drying rack. Many of the pots were bone dry, ready for the kiln.

I shrugged. "Throwing them is the best part."

Ellie's nose wrinkled. "Too messy. And you can't really use them till you fire them, right? Otherwise they'll just break." Mr. Bingle, my cat, weaved between Ellie's legs. She lifted him with the toe of her tennis shoe and scooted him aside.

Ellie sounded a lot like my mom. Mom was always after me to finish what I started. I wiped my muddy hands on my apron and tossed it aside. "What about bolt cutters?"

"Oh!" she said, her eyes lighting up as she jumped back with that thought. "We have bolt cutters at home. I'm going to text Brennan right now and tell him to bring them over."

Ugh. I'd already sunk to asking Brennan for a ride today. No way was I asking him for another favor. And this lock was special somehow. I shook my head. "I don't know about cutting it—"

But Ellie was already punching her thumbs on her phone. "You have a better idea how to sneak into that lock?"

The snakes! I grinned. "In fact, I do."

* * *

Before we even reached the top of the stairs, Ellie's phoned binged with a text back from Brennan: "No way," it read. Ellie shrugged at me, and I pulled the string that opened the hatch to our attic. A wooden ladder tumbled down, barreling out like a captive set free. Dust flew everywhere. Ellie sneezed, a honking blast of a sneeze.

"Bless you," I said to Ellie's back. She was already plowing into the dark abyss of our attic. I peered into the black hole gaping above me. Cool air whooshed out of it like a sigh, an icy yawn from our tired, old home.

I heard Ellie yank the lightbulb chain. "Light's burned out," she yelled down to me. Slivers of insulation twinkled down in tiny shards, coating me like a sprinkling of magic dust.

Something about this gave me a chill, and I didn't think it was the cool air. I knew what my Nina would say: "Climb on up, Jalen! Sometimes you gotta leap before you look." My fingers flew to the pink streak of hair and started twirling.

"Jalen, I can't see a thing," Ellie shouted down. "Come up and show me where this jewelry box is."

I stepped onto the ladder, then climbed the creaky steps and poked my head into the darkness. "Forget it, Ellie. Bad idea. Let's just—"

"Here!" Ellie kicked aside a musty pile of clothes.

Sometimes she had the subtlety of a bulldozer. "This looks like a jewelry box."

"That's it," I said. I nodded at the small black chest she'd unearthed, but I didn't move from my perch on the ladder. "It's really dark up here. Maybe I should get a flashlight."

"C'mon, Jalen," Ellie teased. "Some part of you has to be Sagittarian. I'm going to find out which part."

"My freshly painted toenails?" I asked. I could feel Ellie smirk at me, at my joke about the birthday pedicure she'd given me earlier that day. I sometimes wondered if Ellie and I would be friends if we weren't neighbors. We liked different things, and we had such different families and clothes and houses. Most friends I saw at school looked like twins. Not us.

"Well, it's certainly not your goth-girl tendencies," she said, still rummaging.

I had to grin at that. Problem was, I was goth without even trying: pale skin, black hair. And that natural streak of white shooting through my dark locks. Nina was the only one brave enough to call it what it was: a shock lock. A lock of hair, whitened by shock. My very own public display of grief since I was nine.

And so lately I'd colored it—purple, blue, green, red— you name it. This week it was hot pink. Anything to cover the shock of white.

I climbed fully into the attic, crawling onto a crossbeam

and through a sticky spiderweb. As I did, the spring on the hatch twanged, the ladder shot up, and the trap door of the attic snapped shut behind me.

"Not good," Ellie whispered. The only light came through the slats in the vent on the opposite side of the attic. And we'd obviously disturbed the creatures who lived here, because they scurried into corners with scratches and squeaks.

I pushed down on the hatch, *hard*, but it didn't budge. It was too difficult to push when I couldn't stand up fully in this cramped space.

Panic swelled my throat shut. "Mom's not home yet," I choked out. "Might not be home all night. Who's going to let us out?"

Ellie fished around for something, then her cell phone screen lit up the dark attic like a star. The glow from the phone didn't stretch far and the darkness crowded in, the rafters and beams and piles of stuff stealing from our circle of light whenever they could snatch it from us.

"I'll text Brennan again and tell him he absolutely has to come," Ellie said. " '*Locked in attic*,' " she muttered while typing. " '*Need you*.' "

I swallowed past the lump in my throat. Great. There'd be *no end* to Brennan's teasing now. But he was close, and we didn't have many options. I really hated asking for favors, especially from blowhards like Brennan. And today I'd racked up two. No, three, including the bolt cutters he'd refused to bring us. Now he'd get the pleasure of rescuing us from my mistake.

The cell phone washed the attic in blue light, and I was reminded of those Picasso paintings where everything was gray and blue and lilac. Like the moon, whose murky edges blend into the night.

The phone binged again. *"Ha! Dorks!"* read Brennan's reply.

Panic rose again. "Is he coming or not?" I asked.

Ellie's mouth drew to the side of her face. "Sure. Yeah. I think so. Let's look for that pin."

I could tell Ellie was changing the subject, but there was nothing else to do up here, anyway. I hefted open Nina's ebony jewelry box; it took both hands to lift the ivory-inlaid cover. Nina's pin was right there on top, resting on a pile of pearls, like a mother snake guarding her nest of eggs. Poised to strike, poison at the ready.

The pin was brass, with a single snake twining around a staff. Just as I remembered it, when I'd seen it so long ago.

It was at the hospital, the very hospital where Nina lay, battling cancer tonight. The hospital where I'd been when I was so sick, too. I had been sleeping, lulled into dreamland by beeping machines and the gentle whoosh of the respirator, when my eyes fluttered open. I saw *this*, this pin gleaming over Nina's heart. I'd tried to ask about it, but I couldn't speak, so I pointed at it instead. Nina told me the pin was a symbol of healing. I remember thinking that odd, since snakes usually symbolize death and poison and pain.

"Wow," Ellie sighed over my shoulder, hunched in the cramped attic. Her sigh made me jump; I'd forgotten she was there. "You were right, J. That snake looks just like the two on the lock."

In the blue light of the attic, I held the pin next to the lock. The snake on the pin was an exact match: tiny, intricately carved scales, a diamond-shaped head, a thin, slithery split tongue, emerald-green eyes. Identical snakes, tangled together by fate.

Before I considered the coincidence too much to scare me, I jammed the end of the pin—the point of the staff and the curl of the snake's tail—into the lock on my new book.

It fit.

I turned the key in the lock, and the bodies of the snakes began to untangle. The heads of the snakes twisted away from one another and toward me, sizing me up with blank emerald eyes. The heart of the lock cracked slightly apart.

Click!

It was likely a tiny click, a small, satisfying opening. But to me, that click echoed around this dark space, and I could feel it in my gut.

"It worked!" Ellie said, She shot upright and slammed her head on a rafter. "I can't believe that worked!"

"Me either," I muttered.

The lock had split apart just enough for me to remove the chains binding the book. Which I did, carefully. The cover was warped and crinkly stiff.

I folded the book open, and its spine creaked. A yellowed piece of paper, obviously torn from the book, slid from the pages and floated to the floor of the attic. It was blank. Or wait, no——it wasn't blank? A picture of the lock——the heart-and-snake lock I'd just opened——appeared in the middle of the page.

Ellie nodded eagerly. "Put the lock there," she said, nudging my shoulder. I couldn't see for sure in the dark attic, but I knew her eyes were twinkling with anticipation.

I picked up the lock, key still embedded, and placed it on the piece of paper on the floor. I twisted the lock until its position matched the illustration. The paper and the lock felt almost magnetized, drawn to one another in the pull of attraction, clicking precisely into position. The moment it was aligned, the eyes of all three snakes——the two on the lock and the one on the key——flashed a burst of blinding green light.

Hisssssssssssss! I jerked my hand away. A fine mist rose off the paper, a smoky, swirling, hissing mist. It stank like sulfur, like rotten eggs. The eyes of the snakes dulled but continued to glow, pulsing in the dark attic.

"What *is* that?" Ellie whispered, lifting her sweatshirt collar over her nose. I shook my head, too mesmerized to speak.

The mist began to float and wind and twist to the outer edges of the piece of paper, revealing ink. Moving, liquid-like ink. More snakes. Black-ink snakes, darting and slithering toward one another, first forming letters . . .

Unlock it.

And then a chart.

The ink soaked into the paper, and I saw: It was a zodiac chart, round like the sun, divided into equal parts, one for each horoscope sign.

The mist cleared, the hissing faded, the pulsing green eyes lowered to a dull glow. But the sulfur smell remained, stinging my eyes and throat. The lock, the paper, the chart remained as well.

Something was odd about this chart, aside from the fact that it had literally appeared from mist. Nina was a staunch believer in astrology, so I'd seen plenty of zodiac charts, divided into the twelve horoscope signs. This one was different.

How? I blinked at the chart, trying to figure out what was off. I started at the top of the chart and counted clockwise around: *Aries the Ram, Taurus the Bull, Gemini the Twins, Cancer the Crab, Leo the Lion, Virgo the Maiden, Libra the Scales, Scorpio the Scorpion, Ophiuchus the Snake* . . .

Ophiuchus? O-*what?!*

I blinked but counted through the remaining signs: *Sagittarius the Archer, Capricorn the Goat, Aquarius the Water Bearer, Pisces the Fish.*

This zodiac chart had thirteen signs. Thirteen, not twelve. I counted twice to make sure.

"Thirteen signs . . ." I muttered to the paper. A new zodiac. Of course, I didn't believe in horoscopes or zodiacs or astrological signs of any sort—what a load of hoo. I only read this stuff for Nina. And yet, staring at that new, crowded zodiac chart, a zing shot down my spine.

"A sign between Scorpio and Sagittarius," I said, studying the thirteen-sign chart but still refusing to touch the paper. I located my birth date on the outside of the wheel. "According to this, my new sign is O-however-you-say-it."

Ellie flipped through the brittle pages of the book.

"Hey, that sign is listed in here." She read the description of the sign:

"*'Ophiuchus (o-PHEW-cuss), the snake. November 30—December 17. Ophiuchus, thou art overlooked. Thou hast a hunger, then, that thou strivest to fill with knowledge, and thou seekest the truth above all. Because of this, thou art a favourite among authority figures. However, know that with hunger comes jealousy; the jealousy of the hungered cannot be matched. Too, this black blood masks a vicious secretive streak, so that thou art wildly misinterpreted. Because of this, thou lackest trust and commitment. And yet, thy friends art thy lifeline; thou definest thine own identity through the lens of others. Should thou overcomest thine thy crippling anger, thine healer's hands have the power to revive lost souls.'*"

This was me.

I hovered above the paper, studying this new zodiac chart—this *ancient* zodiac chart, according to what Ellie read in *The Keypers of the Zodiack*. There were actually thirteen constellations in the path our planet took around the sun. Thirteen signs, not twelve.

" '*When the Babylonians first developed a zodiac chart,*' " Ellie read, " '*they rightly included all thirteen constellations. The twelve-sign zodiac evolved later from the Greeks. The Greeks based their zodiac on the Legend of the Twelve Labours of Hercules. In this myth, Hercules had angered King Eurystheus, and the king demanded that Hercules perform Twelve Labours, or Challenges, to spare his life.*

" '*As Hercules achieved victory after victory, he honored his Challengers by casting them into the heavens as constellations. These twelve groupings of stars, the Greeks believed, were given the power to control our personalities.*' "

Ellie continued reading. " '*Over time, the twelve-sign zodiac became the standard. The thirteenth sign, Ophiuchus, was forever lost.*' "

A lost sign.

"Total crap," Ellie said. She slammed the book shut and looked over my shoulder at the thirteen-sign chart. "There is no way I'm not a Libra. I mean, now I'm suddenly a Virgo? No way."

I half smiled. Ellie took this horoscope stuff way too seriously. But it was intriguing. Wedging a thirteenth sign into the zodiac meant *all* the dates of the astrological calendar would shift. This would change the horoscope signs of my family members, my friends. The sign that we'd defined ourselves with, aligned ourselves with, now suddenly different? I have to admit, I liked the sound of all that chaos.

"And Brennan? What would his new sign be? His birthday's August first," Ellie said.

"I know when his birthday is."

The ancient chart was difficult to see in the dull blue light of the cell phone, and the eyes of the snakes were now only slightly brighter than glow-in-the-dark stars. I'd need more light to read the chart.

I nudged the paper with my toe. Nothing happened. I tapped it quickly, lightly with one finger. Nothing.

Finally, I took a deep breath and picked up the paper. The lock clung to it, like it had been glued to the spot where I'd placed it.

I crossed to the other side of the attic, ignoring the scuffling and hissing of furry things, and opened the vent like a shutter, letting in light from the full moon.

I lifted the thin piece of paper with both hands. It became almost transparent against the moonlight. The words *"Unlock it"* just above the heart-and-snake lock, just above the thirteen-sign chart.

Unlock it.

It was irresistible. I reached up and turned the key in the lock one more notch.

The heart cracked completely in two, a fully broken heart. The eyes of the snakes flashed, filling the room with green lightning. The paper turned into hissing mist and disappeared, surrounding me, enveloping me, trapping me. The lock clattered to the floor.

My axis tilted, my ears buzzed, and a thought blazed through my head like fire before my skull smacked against the floor of the attic:

I am an Ophiuchus.

At the time, I didn't know that everyone would change because of me.

That everything I loved about everyone I knew would vanish.

That all that chaos would leap right off that page.

Had I known that, I never would've opened the lock.

3

Are you okay?"

The question echoed in my head. I blinked, then blinked again. A drumbeat of pain *poundpoundpounded* through my skull with my pulse.

Brennan snapped his fingers at me. The darkness receded, the light blinded me. I was standing in the hallway of the second story of my house, no longer in the attic. The hatch door was open, the ladder was down, and cold air wafted in from above. My whole body tingled, like when your arm falls asleep, then slowly prickles back to life.

"What?" My voice sounded far away. Buried. "I thought you weren't coming."

"Of course I came! You were locked in an attic." Brennan looked upset. "Are you okay? You guys were up there for a while. Want me to make you some hot chocolate?"

"So you can poison it?" My fingers shot up to cover my mouth. Had I really said that?

But Brennan's face sank into a frown, rather than snapped into the snarl I'd expected. Odd.

I looked down at myself, holding *The Keypers of the Zodiack* in one hand, Nina's pin clasped to my T-shirt over my heart. Freshly painted toenails. It was all the same, except I was somehow wearing that pin. Still, *something* was different. More—colorful? The world now seemed painted in oranges and yellows and reds. A Matisse, not a Picasso. The sun, not the moon. It reminded me of the time when I'd been in the hospital, when I'd seen the world though fevery eyes.

My pulse raced. "You guys didn't—black out or anything just then? How did we get down here? How long were we up there? Where is the lock? Why am I wearing this pin?" Even as I was asking the questions, I wanted my mouth to stop talking. But I couldn't. Stop talking. I moved my jawbone around to try and open my blocked ears.

Ellie cocked her head at me, her blond ponytail swinging. She didn't have a ponytail earlier, did she? "Are you okay, Jalen? Maybe we should go sit down."

She took *The Keypers of the Zodiack* from my hand and led me downstairs to the overstuffed couch in our living room. She sat down placed the book on the cushion beside her, and patted the seat. So calm. No animation—why was she acting like this? Was I really hurt and they just weren't telling me? I scanned my body—no cuts, no blood, no bruises.

Mr. Bingle jumped into her lap and started purring. Ellie smiled and stroked him, twining the fingers of her left hand in his orange fur. Her right hand flew to her mouth, and she gnawed off the electric-green fingernail polish with her teeth.

"When did you start biting your nails?" The words clogged my throat.

Ellie looked down at the almost-gone polish. "This junky polish is just awful. Honestly, Jalen. Why did you let me go out in public wearing this?"

I blinked. Ellie had squealed when she saw that polish in the drugstore two days ago. She had been thrilled, because it was "the exact color of june bugs."

After a too-long moment of silence (because normally, Ellie was a silence killer), she asked in a squeaky voice, "Feeling better, Jalen?" She lifted one of Mr. Bingle's paws in a silly mock wave.

"Ellie, you're allergic to cats."

"What? No, I'm not."

"Hmm. I always thought that was a lie." I bit my lip, like that could help me unsay those words. Sure, I'd suspected Ellie's "cat allergies" were just a deep dislike of cats, but I'd never *say* that. Until . . . now? Ellie looked both hurt and confused.

I started to feel dizzy. I slumped onto the couch next to Ellie, sank into the cozy cushions. "You didn't black out? Just now?" I felt around on my head for a tender place, a bump or a bruise. Nothing. I remembered collapsing to the floor of the attic, my head leading the way.

Brennan paced the vintage living room rug. He looked at me with what appeared to be real concern. But you didn't just *forget* a rivalry like ours, not over something silly like being locked in an attic. No—he was up to something. I suspected they both were, acting like this. But what?

"I'm worried about you, Jalen," he said. "You don't look so hot, no offense. Do you want me to call your mom?"

My mom? *No offense?* "No," I whispered. "She's with my Nina."

Just the mention of my Nina caused Brennan's forehead to wrinkle in pity. Untouched by tragedy, he was. And now, suddenly *now*, he cared? What was going on here? It felt like a joke, and I didn't like it one bit.

I steeled myself for what I knew would come next: the sting of tears in my eyes, the tingling of the tip of my nose, the tightening of my throat—all my usual reactions when Brennan made fun of me. But none of that happened.

I cracked my knuckles. Ellie cringed next to me. *I cracked my knuckles?* And then, what I *wasn't* doing became just as obvious as what I *was* doing. I wasn't twisting my streaked hair into knots. I snagged a lock and drew it across my face.

"What in the—" I flipped around and perched on my knees on the couch. I shook my head at my reflection in the dark window.

It was gone! The shock lock—*missing!* Filled in, somehow, with black hair, just like the rest.

It was like nothing had ever hurt me. As if my past had been glossy smooth. I had nothing to show for my pain.

Did I still have the pain?

I swallowed to try and stop the dizzy spins, and then I realized—the buzzing sound was our antique doorbell, not my head. BZZZZZT! BZZZ-BZZZ-BZZZZT!

I crawled off the couch, stumbling toward the door. Ellie grabbed my wrist. "Jalen, don't answer that! Your mom's not home!" Her eyes were wide with fear.

"What?" I shook my head to dislodge her words from my ears. Ellie afraid? This little act was really starting to bug me. I yanked my wrist free. "Really, who could it be?"

"Who could what be?" said Brennan.

Ellie and I both cocked our heads at him. "The door," I said. "You know, the one with the ringing doorbell?" *Whoa.* That came out way more sarcastic than I'd meant it to. I shook it off and crossed the entryway.

Through the cut glass front door, I could see someone on the front stoop. As I swung the door open, I got a better view: a woman, maybe teens or early twenties, with leaves in her hair. Leaves! And she was wearing—was I seeing this right?—a toga. A sheet, wrapped and draped around her body, belted with a shiny gold rope.

Hmmph, New Orleans, I thought. But it wasn't the season for Mardi Gras costumes. And something about this woman didn't click. She wasn't some kind of caricature dreamed up by the krewes who organized the parades.

No. She didn't appear to be playing pretend.

Her eyes—what was it? Her eyes were black pupils, no color. Empty, infinite, midnight eyes.

"See?" Brennan said over my shoulder. "No one's there. I really think we oughta call your mom, Jalen."

Ellie pushed her brother's arm. "Don't be rude!" she whispered sharply.

"What?" Brennan threw his arms out, palms up.

But I was still too disoriented after staring into those empty eyes to snap at Brennan. "Sorry," I said to the lady in the toga. "We don't have any beads for you to throw in your parade." I started to ease the door shut. She placed her foot in the crack of the door.

"Jalen Jones," she said. Her voice crackled like a snake's rattle.

My stomach clenched into a fist. "How do you know my name?" I pushed the door harder, but her foot was still lodged in the crack. And it didn't appear that she'd move it anytime soon. My eyes widened. I turned to Ellie and Brennan in a silent plea of help.

Brennan placed a hand on my shoulder. "Jalen, close the door and come back inside. I'm really getting worried about—"

"I can't!" I yelled at him. "Her foot is in the door, Brennan!" I shoved the door harder, harder, but it wouldn't budge.

Brennan's forehead wrinkled. "Whose foot?"

"Hers!" Ellie pointed at the sandal wedged in the door. She cupped her hands around her mouth and, nearing hysterics, started yelling, "Go away! I'm calling the police! I know karate!" (She doesn't.) I kept pushing the door, smashing the foot, but the woman never uttered a word.

"Jalen," the woman repeated again, sharper this time. Yet she sounded calm, very much unlike the scene on this side of the door. "You called me."

"What?" My voice was high. I fought to keep it steady. "What do you mean, called? I haven't called anyone!"

"Called who, Jalen?" Brennan asked, his head whipping back and forth from me to Ellie. "Ellie, what's going on? Did you guys call me over here to play a trick on me? Because ha-ha, enough's enough."

Two sets of fingers slithered around the door, gripped it, and pushed. Even though I threw my whole weight against it, the woman flung open the door with ease.

Brennan's eyes widened, but I could see he focused beyond the lady in the toga, into the dark night. He didn't see her. "Whoa," he muttered.

The stranger shoved into my home, slammed the door, and blocked the exit. She reached over her shoulder and flicked the dead bolt with a twist of her fingers. She never once removed her blank-black eyes from us.

"What is your business with Ophiuchus?" she growled.

My mouth went dry. Ophiuchus. She knew something.

I tried to signal to Ellie and Brennan to run for the back door. The lady stepped toward me, and I couldn't help but take a step back. She fumbled around inside the pouch strapped across her chest. My mind assumed the worst: She was grabbing a gun! A knife! A *something*!

I snatched a pottery bowl holding keys and sunglasses off the entry table and smashed it over her head. I looked down at the fragment still in my hand in amazement. *How about me!* My heart pounded in my throat at this newfound fire.

The lady shook her glossy black hair, flinging pottery shards. As she did, she pulled a metal nail file from her pouch. She pointed it at me, touching me lightly between the eyes with the tip. I tasted bile.

"You? You're Jalen? You're a child." She seemed to pause, then she flipped the file between her fingers like a drumstick and began filing her nails, *zip zip zip.* Bone-chillingly fast, the file sawed.

She was filing her nails?

"Who are you?" My pointed voice surprised me.

"Jalen?" Brennan asked. He stepped toward me, too close to the woman. Ellie jumped forward and yanked him back.

The lady flitted her black eyes over me, over my friends. "Why did you summon us? What is your business with Ophiuchus?"

The knots in my muscles jerked tighter. "I don't know what you mean. How do you know my name?" I asked. I tried to be strong, but my voice wavered.

"Oh, look at that. She's scared!" The lady leaned close to my face, too close. With her sharpened pinkie fingernail, she stroked a line from the outer corner of my eye to my jawbone, the path a tear would take.

"Already, Jalen, with the fear?" she whispered. "I'm afraid you're not going to last very long at all."

She stood tall and snapped the nail file into the palm of her hand. I jumped.

"You think you can just unlock Ophiuchus and *not* unleash the fury of the heavens?" she demanded.

Words were trapped in my throat. I grew hot. "I—"

"You think it'll be so easy to gain that kind of power, Jalen?"

"I—"

"You think the other twelve are just going to let you saunter in and pluck Ophiuchus's stone from the heavens, Jalen?"

I blinked. "Other twelve?"

The woman sneered at me. "Allow me to introduce myself. I'm Gemini," she said, extending her hand genteelly, like I might kiss it. Her tone changed so abruptly, it was like talking to two people.

"Like the zodiac sign?" Ellie squeaked.

Brennan huffed. "Zodiac? Is that what this is all about?" He stomped away from us, back into the living room, and picked up *The Keypers of the Zodiack* off the couch. He shivered.

Brennan's eyes were lowered, looking at the book as he returned. "You two were over here reading this, and you got all spooked out, and so you decided to——" He raised his eyes.

"Holy——what is *that?*" Brennan scrambled backward, away from the person calling herself Gemini, and tripped over the rug. He landed with a thud on his tailbone, the palm of his hand crunching on a shard of pottery. A pool of blood quickly spilled beneath it. *Now* he saw her?

Gemini eyed him coolly. "Aren't you a simple one?" she cooed at him, smoothing her sleek black hair. "It's a good thing you're not the one seeking Ophiuchus. You'd be pulp." But she offered her hand, helping him stand. She pulled a cloth from her pouch for his cut. This woman was manic.

Her black gaze turned steely again and she whipped it toward me, sending a chill to my fingertips. "Yes. Well. *Jalen*. If you're hunting Ophiuchus, you should be on your way. Consider this your warning."

She leaned in toward me again, black eyes narrowed. "And I won't be so *polite* the next time our paths cross. No offense. You understand it's my duty to do whatever it takes to stop you. Now, you really should get going."

My head was spinning, trying to compute all of this. "Going?"

Gemini sighed. "On your search? Though I must say, looking at you with your mouth hanging open like that, I'm not certain you're up for it. You'll be easy meat to those Keepers." She grabbed my chin and shook it. My brain rattled.

I snapped my head back to escape her grasp. "Meat? I'm not going anywhere."

"Yes, Jalen. It's time for the games to begin. Just remember that those who seek great power pay a great price."

Tears swam in my eyes, but somehow I managed to choke down a sob. "This is some kind of mistake," my voice said. "I don't understand. I don't want power."

Gemini blinked, her brow furrowed. Her black hair was shiny sleek, her red lips full. Movie-star gorgeous. She leaned close to me, looking deep into my eyes, like she was reading my soul.

"You're not like the other Challengers," she whispered. "You really *don't* know." Then, almost panicked, she added, "You have *no idea* what you've unleashed on the universe, do you?"

My head twitched *no.*

"You don't seek Ophiuchus's power?"

No again.

Her shoulders fell. She paused before speaking. "I'll need to go with you. You can't do this alone." Chill bumps raced over my skin. I wasn't going anywhere with this roller-coaster ride.

"That book. Your book. *The Keypers of the Zodiack?*" Gemini asked. I nodded at Brennan, one bloody hand clenched around the scrap of cloth, his other hand still clutching the book. It struck me: After he held the book, he could see her, could hear her. The book somehow unlocked our sight of this maniac. The back of my neck prickled.

"How much of it did you read?" Gemini demanded.

Do I lie? Pretend I know everything about her? It didn't seem like a good idea. Truth seemed smarter. "Not a lot."

Gemini's face seemed to soften a moment, but she quickly locked that away behind a scowl. She shook her head and straightened her toga with sharp tugs.

"Jalen." Gemini's voice was level. "You have unlocked Ophiuchus, the thirteenth sign of the zodiac. These personality changes you and your friends have experienced?" She lifted a single eyebrow, allowing her words to sink in.

Personality changes? Ellie and Brennan had been acting weird, yes. And I certainly felt different. To put it mildly. But personality *changes*?

"They're just the start of your problems," Gemini said. "But know this: If you don't come with me, all of the changes, across the globe, will become permanent."

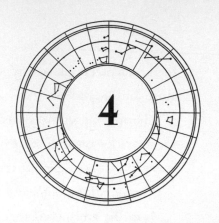

4

I thought about what this person, Gemini, said for a moment: *across the globe*.

"You're saying . . . everyone on earth has changed."

Gemini nodded. "All humans possess a new horoscope sign now that Ophiuchus has been awoken." She flipped the nail file in her fingers. I bristled, preparing to feel the sharp point between my eyes again, boring into my brain. But she tucked it away, inside her pouch, rather than sawing it across my flesh. "And with that, everyone's personality has shifted."

No, I misunderstood. There's no way everyone on earth had a personality switch.

Gemini crossed to the dark window, like she was searching for something. She didn't have a reflection in the glass. I shivered. "You must find Ophiuchus and cast her back into the heavens to right this wrong, Jalen."

"Find Ophiuchus," I said. "To fix everyone's personalities." This wasn't happening. This woman—this *thing* that required the touch of a book to even be seen?—was really starting to scare me. "Right."

Gemini turned away from the window and crossed to me. Looking into her stare was like looking into a black hole and was just as much of a trap.

"Ophiuchus is with the one who needs healing."

Had she whispered that, or had I imagined it? I looked over Gemini's shoulder at once-brash Brennan now biting his bottom lip, at Ellie gnawing her fingernails. It appeared no one heard that but me. If I heard it at all.

Her black eyes flashed, a spark of green shooting through them like a comet. My mind sprang to the snakes on the lock, the pin. My hand instinctively covered Nina's pin over my heart.

Nina. If what this woman was saying was true . . . No. It couldn't be. What *was* she saying? That my mom, my Nina— now had different personalities? I didn't like the sound of that. Not one bit.

"I want to call my mother," I said. I waggled my fingers at Ellie. "Let me see your cell phone."

Ellie fished the cell phone from her jeans pocket and passed it to me. Mom usually answered on the first ring. But this time it rang and rang and rang before I got sent to voice mail. Twice. Finally, on the third try, my mother answered.

"Jalen!" she shrieked.

My stomach leaped into my throat. "Mom?"

"Jalen!" she choked out. "Oh, Jalen, honey. It's bad. Bad!" I could barely understand her between her gulping sobs. My mom never cried. Never, not even when my dad had disappeared.

I realized I was blinking back tears. "Nina? Is she okay?" I heard Nina moaning, groaning in the background. "Is that her?" I asked too loudly. "Is she okay?"

Each cry of my mom's ratcheted up my fear. My mother's tears and my Nina's moans came through the phone in a chorus of pain.

"Mrs. Jones," said a voice in the background. It was muffled, but I could hear snatches of the conversation around my mother's sobs. "Calm down . . . not helping matters . . . be strong for your mother." It must've been the nurse.

"My *mother-in-law*," my mom wailed to the voice. I'd never heard her correct that before. "You-you can't make that moaning stop?"

"No, ma'am," the nurse in the background said. "Can't explain it . . . mother-in-law . . . given up all her fight. You and your family . . . think about saying good-bye."

"Mom!" I shouted, but she didn't hear me over the sound of her own crying. "Mom, what do they mean, say good-bye? Mom?"

"Jalen! I can't do this anymore. I'm—I'm leaving."

The phone clicked dead.

＊ ＊ ＊

Saying good-bye. To Nina? Rather, to a woman who didn't *sound* like my Nina. Not at all.

I could hardly breathe. I dropped Ellie's cell phone.

My Nina was brave, bold, and beautiful, even battling breast cancer. But now—now, it seemed, she was in so much pain. Had she been in pain when I talked to her earlier? My heart sobbed at the thought of it.

Nina was the one at home when I got off the school bus because my mom had to work long hours. She thought everything was better with a plate of warm chocolate-chip cookies. And she said, "thank heavens!" all the time in this way that made you think she had some personal angel up there, hammering it all out for her.

Nina was my dad's mom, but she treated my mom like her own blood. My mom and I hadn't had a normal conversation without Nina in the room in four years. After my dad disappeared, my mom hardened, like she was clanking around in a suit of armor. In fact, my mom didn't say he "disappeared." She never said otherwise, but I suspected Mom thought Daddy left us when things got tough.

But Nina believed differently. Nina had tethered Mom and me to earth after Daddy's accident, rather than allowing us to drift up and away.

And now Mom was *leaving*? Leaving the hospital? That woman *wasn't* my mom. My throat squeezed shut.

I'd thought having a too-tough mom was such a horrible thing. But a quitter mom? No. She was the only parent I had left. She can't just check out. Not now. Not on what might be Nina's last night on earth!

"I have to go to the hospital," I whispered. I cleared my throat. "I have to be with Nina. She can't die—I mean, she can't *be* alone."

Ellie laid a gentle hand on my shoulder. "But the hospital rules say—"

"Oh, forget the hospital rules, Ellie!" Once I said it—forget the rules!—I felt my new fire inside kick off a few sizzling sparks. Felt the sparks lift me higher. The hospital let me in when I was their *patient*, for heaven's sake. They'll let me in now. Forget the rules! Forget them! "I'm going."

Gemini nodded. "Yes. You should get going. And I'm coming with you."

I narrowed my eyes at this twisted lady. "No, thanks."

Gemini grabbed the front of my T-shirt and twisted it, slammed me against a wall, lifted me off the floor. I gagged, the cords in my neck straining, my feet dangling. "You don't understand," she growled. "You can't do this alone."

Do I knee her or calm her down? I wanted to knee her, but she had an obvious physical advantage.

"Easy, lady," I said. My brain churned. "You don't want to hurt me. I'm the one who has to find Ophiuchus, remember?"

Believe it or not, that craziness worked. She nodded

and set me down, adjusting her toga with sharp tugs and tucks.

I bit my lip, partly to keep it from quivering, partly to hold back a stream of cuss words. No way was this lady coming with me to see my Nina. We'd have to ditch her— and soon.

5

I turned to Brennan. "Can you—"

He already had his keys out. "Of course." He crossed to the front door and opened it for me. Brennan. Offering to drive *and* opening doors. I shivered at the creepiness of it.

Brennan handed *The Keypers of the Zodiack* to Ellie, who hesitantly took it. She tucked it into her messenger bag. We walked into the night and saw a stout guy peering into Brennan's truck. His hands were cupped around his eyes, pressed against the glass.

"Truck's not for sale, bub," Brennan called to him.

The man turned, his jowls jiggling, and flashed a brilliant smile. His tailored suit was sharp as paper. "What makes you think I'd buy that heap of junk, anyway?"

Gemini turned to Ellie. "Let me see the book." Ellie took a step back.

Gemini harrumphed, waggled her fingers. Ellie swallowed and handed over *The Keypers of the Zodiack*. Gemini flipped through the pages until she found the one she was looking for, then thrust the open book at me. "Read that."

I read it out loud.

> "*'Taurus, the bull. May 14–June 19. Taurus, thou dost not possess an easy mind to alter. Stubborn and willful art thou. Despite thine obstinate nature, thou art quite incapable of deceit. Too, thou art careful, reliable, trustworthy—a steady and staid friend. No one knows how to enjoy life more than a Taurus, nor cannot a soul be better at leisure—thou art the Master of Leisure. Be warned: Greed has steeped into thy very bones. With thy creativity and well-laid plans, thou can risest to the top, where thou feelest thou rightfully belong. Just be sure thou dost not climb so high thou losest sight of those beneath thee, Taurus. Strong blows can come from below.'*"

I blinked, unsure of what it meant. "Okay. Sure. Thanks." This lady was really creeping me out.

The gentleman tugged at his jacket lapels, the silk hanky in his breast pocket gleaming. "Jalen?" he asked. "Oh, my! You're a child!" He tossed his head back and laughed a booming laugh. He straightened, suddenly, and sucked his teeth with his tongue.

How did this guy know my name, too? *Oh, no,* I thought. *They're a team!* My heart raced. I wasn't sure the three of us could take the two of them, but I'd sure as heck give it a shot.

"But honestly, Jalen," he said. "You couldn't have called me to New Orleans during Mardi Gras? Now *that's* my kind of indulgence."

His beady eyes whipped toward Gemini. She extended her hand as she had before, her wrist arched like a cat's back. He planted a wet kiss on her creamy flesh.

"And you," he murmured, glaring up at her. His stare was filled with passion, but I couldn't tell if that passion was made of love or hate. "Always a pleasure, but my, my, my, what a surprise."

Gemini swallowed and wiped the back of her slobbery hand across her toga.

I looked at Gemini. "Who is he?"

The gentleman's laughter increased. His diamond-stud earring flashed under the streetlamp. "Oh, the naïveté is such a nice touch!" He collected himself and clenched his fist, showcasing a thick, domed class ring. I got the message: That ring would *hurt* in a punch. My eyes flitted around for the closest thing that could be used as a weapon.

"This your house?" the man asked, jerking his meaty head at my home. His neck wobbled. Based on the way his lip snarled, I could tell he thought it was beneath him to live in such a dump.

My anger burned. "This house is pre–Civil War, buddy. Much older than you are." Listen to me! I've never talked to adults that way. I've never talked to *anyone* that way.

"Is that so?" The gentleman hooted with laughter. "Oh, you really know how to play up the whole kid angle, don't you? Priceless." He snapped out of his joviality again. "But it won't make me take it any easier on you."

And then he collapsed. His body disappeared into a low cloud of mist, as if melting into fog. The mist stunk, just like the mist that rose off the paper earlier this evening. Smelly, like rotten eggs.

Ellie screamed. Somewhere in the dark night a dog barked. The mist curled and rose and out of it came a form, a shape, gnarled and hurling, growing ever bigger, ever larger, until it reached its full height—six feet or so. It snorted, hooves clicking on the street's pavement, and stepped under the streetlamp.

Massive pointed horns. Thick skull. Shoulders like a brick wall. Trim waist. And an enormous gold ring, now in its nose.

A bull.

A bull rose from the mist.

Under the giant creaking oaks, under the dangling Spanish moss, I locked eyes with the bull that stood between us and Brennan's truck. I was frozen with disbelief. I tried refocusing my eyes. Still a bull. No longer a man.

Ellie turned to run back into the house, but with one mighty leap, the bull was over and around us, blocking us from my home.

"The truck bed!" Brennan yelled. The three of us scrambled into the back of the pickup truck, while Gemini stood in the middle of the yard, where we'd originally stopped.

"Lady, come on!" I yelled to Gemini, but she didn't budge. I didn't have much time to consider it. The bull was readying himself for attack.

From the dim lights on the front porch, I could see the bull's flanks twitch, signaling his preparation. He snorted. Puffs of air shot from his black-pit nostrils in the cool night. The bull scratched his hind legs, lowered his thick skull, and charged.

The bull battered the side of Brennan's truck with his mighty horns. My head snapped back. It felt like the punch he'd promised earlier. Metal groaned, crunched.

The bull twisted free from the steel. He began bucking and writhing, attacking the truck with swift kicks and long horns. Brennan's truck was crushed like a tin can under the impact. We three lurched backward.

The bull backed up, never removing his black eyes from us. He scratched the ground with his left front hoof, pointed his horns at us, and charged again. Metal creaked and glass shattered as the bull bashed the truck with twice the impact of the previous blow. The hit sent us flailing. Brennan stumbled over the side of the truck bed. His T-shirt snagged on a tool hook, leaving him dangling a foot above the ground. Totally vulnerable to attack.

The bull must've sensed this vulnerability, because he circled the truck, snorting and snarling. He saw Brennan on the opposite side from where he'd been focusing his attack. The bull twitched his ears and adjusted his left horn, its point focused on Brennan like a laser. He made a guttural noise, the sound of fury, and charged.

Ellie and I grabbed Brennan. We managed to haul him back into the truck before the bull struck his mighty blow. I fell on top of a pile of sharp tools, and pain shot up my arm. The bull must've pierced the gas tank on that charge, because the scent of gasoline burned my throat.

The bull yanked and pulled, his long left horn trapped. Each yank was a jarring jerk forward. I thought he might be stuck, that we might be able to make a run for it. But with a ferocious snort, he freed himself from the tangle of metal and rust.

And now, he was really mad.

The bull's black eyes flashed, and in a heartbeat, he bounded on top of the cab of the truck. He crushed the roof with his massive hooves, shattered the windows with his bulking weight. I turned my head to protect my eyes from flying shards of glass when I saw them.

The bolt cutters. Brennan had brought them after all.

The bull towered above us, him on the truck cab, us in the truck bed. He marched and crushed and finally aimed his left horn at us again, readying himself for the final blow.

He snorted hot breath so close I could feel its steaminess. His tail snapped like a flag. He leaped.

I swooped down, snatched up the bolt cutters. I lifted them over my head, shouting to boost my strength. I'd never killed anything before—an ant, sure, and some spiders—but this? I reminded myself that this was no ordinary bull; *this* bull had once been a man. *This* bull had risen from mist.

Strong blows can come from below. I hoped Taurus's horoscope was accurate.

I screamed my throat raw as I stabbed the bull in the neck. I prepared myself for the shower of warm blood, the collapsing of the massive beast on top of me.

But instead of crushing us, the beast dissolved. He burst into a trail of light that shot into the sky like a firework. It was blinding and brilliant and bewildering. He snorted and bucked into the skies in the shape of a bull.

Plunk. Next to my foot, a smooth, flat stone dropped. It was about the size of a billiard ball, and it was deep green. A brilliant emerald.

Ellie crouched behind me, her arms over her head. She peeked an eye open. "What happened?"

"I'm not sure." I tapped the stone with the toe of my sneaker. My foot snapped back, like I expected the stone to morph into something dangerous and snorting, too.

"Hey! What are you kids doing to that truck?" a voice yelled.

Brennan, Ellie, and I whipped around to see a shiny black car—a fancy, old-people car, like a Lincoln or something—in the road next to us. The two men inside glared at us through the open driver's window. I realized what the driver saw: three kids standing in a destroyed truck, one—me—holding bolt cutters.

Gemini was suddenly beside the truck. "Tell him you found it this way," she instructed. If what I thought was true, then these men couldn't see or hear her, not unless they touched the book.

I dropped the bolt cutters with a thunk. "We found it this way." I choked out the lie like it tasted awful. I'd never had a problem with half truths before, but even this small lie hurt.

The driver reached down inside his car, picked up a cell phone, and started dialing.

Gemini was now in the truck with us, holding the mysterious emerald stone out toward me. "Take it—quickly!"

I shook my head, but she thrust it at me. "Take it!" she hissed. I did. "Lift it to the sky," she said. I lifted the stone; it had the heft of a billiard ball, too. I wondered if the men in the car could see the stone, if they wondered why I lifted my hands to the stars.

"Say this: *'Sic itur ad astra,'*" Gemini said.

" *'Sic itur ad astra,'*" I repeated.

The stone dissolved in my hands. It felt like Pop Rocks

on my skin, fizzling and bubbly. It shot into the sky, just as the bull had, trailing behind it a fantastic, fiery tail.

We were all so dazzled by the display that we almost forgot about the men in the car next to us. But Gemini brought us back down to earth, back to the bashed, rusting truck, to the police that were likely on the way.

"To the bus stop," she instructed. "Run!"

We jumped out of the twisted metal heap that was once a truck and ran.

As we did, a single zip sliced the air just next to my ear. A stick arced ahead of me and lodged in the dirt. It was so fast—a blur, really—that it was only after I saw the stiff feathers on the tail of the thing that I felt hot pain on the side of my head.

My ear had been sliced. Bright red blood poured out, matting my hair, staining my T-shirt. My heart pounded in my throat, pumped spurts of blood from the cut in my ear.

Those men had shot an *arrow*?

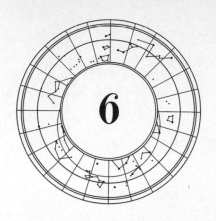

6

Ellie, Brennan, and I ran through several backyards to the bus stop. And the best luck we'd had yet fell on us. The men in the car didn't seem to follow. Then again, neither did Gemini.

The bus wasn't at the stop yet, so we hurried under the clear-plastic shelter, pockmarked with posters announcing jazz festivals and dog grooming. None of us spoke. I think we were in shock. And we must've looked as bad as we felt, because a guy with long blond hair sitting on the bench wrinkled his brow at us. "You guys alright? That cut of yours looks nasty."

I reached up to touch my ear and wished I hadn't, the way the pain sliced through me. My T-shirt was a mess. I'd have to find a new one.

We nodded. "Yes, sir," Brennan said.

The guy glared at us, and my skin prickled. But a grin smeared across his face. "Dude," he said. "Do *not* call me sir.

Makes me feel old." He began tapping out a drumbeat on his knees. A tuba case rested by his feet, covered with stickers from all the local dives he'd played. A musician headed into the city tonight for a gig.

I lifted the corner of my mouth, giving him as much of a smile as I could muster. "You got it."

Brennan turned back to us, now that our silence had been broken. "Um—what was that?" he whispered sharply into our huddle.

I sucked in a wavery breath, not sure myself. A tear slid down Ellie's cheek. Her pocket buzzed, and she looked at the text on her cell. "It's Mom. She wants to know where we are. I think we should go home, B. Jalen, come with us."

Ellie's mom, sending a where-are-you text? Never happens. I shook my head. I didn't like the sound of it, of Ellie and Brennan now having the protective parents.

Gemini was suddenly beside me in our huddle. I jumped.

"Where have you been? And what was that—that *bull*?" I demanded. I looked over Gemini's shoulder to make sure the musician couldn't hear us. No point in making him think we were totally nutty.

Gemini eyed my bloody ear and handed me some gauze from her pouch. Then she whisked out her metal nail file and began sawing away. I wanted to snatch the stupid thing and sling it into the sewer grate.

Gemini must've sensed my fire. She cleared her throat,

tucked away her nail file, and began twisting her manicured fingers in her glossy black hair. For a moment, I missed that I used to do that, too. My jittery fingers took to dabbing at my ear instead. Pain shot through me to my toes.

"When Jalen called Ophiuchus, she called all the Keepers of the Zodiac," Gemini whispered. I wondered why, since that musician obviously couldn't hear her. "Every horoscope sign. Their job is not only to guide decisions and shape personalities. They have sworn to protect and hide Ophiuchus."

"Why?" Brennan asked. Yes, why. Like *why* are we here, *why* the zodiac signs, *why* us?

Gemini paused, like she was trying to figure out what exactly to tell us. I felt my eyes narrow at her.

"Ophiuchus has great power," she said. "The power to heal. Power that humans seek and will abuse if discovered. Power to . . . *alter* humanity. The other twelve Keepers? Nothing but mere sky matter without their loyal humans. They—*we*—have sworn to battle anyone who unlocks Ophiuchus. Anyone who knows how to awaken Ophiuchus is seen by the other twelve as a threat to the order of the universe."

"Jalen," Ellie whispered.

"Jalen," Gemini agreed.

Hearing my name mentioned in whispers like that, just like my dad's name had been mentioned in whispers for months after he had disappeared, made a little of the light inside me die.

"Jalen will have to defeat each Keeper, just as Hercules did in the Twelve Labours," Gemini continued. "It is their goal to eliminate you, Jalen. You are the Challenger. Only once you are eliminated do they feel they can rest, only then do they believe that the universe is safe. You must battle them if you, *ahem* . . ." She paused.

"If you wish to live. And congratulations. You just defeated Taurus. Only eleven more Challenges to go. Yours truly included, of course." She tapped at the base of her throat with a shiny fingernail and raised an eyebrow at me.

I looked over Gemini's shoulder at the musician, still drumming on his knees under the bus shelter. He looked at his watch, then up the empty street for the bus. What I wouldn't give to be only worried about the stinking bus right now.

Gemini sighed. "The Keepers don't know you mean no harm, Jalen. Most other Challengers, you see . . ." Her words trailed off. She cleared her throat.

"Your goal is to find Ophiuchus—and quickly," she continued. "If earth passes out of the House of Ophiuchus before you find the sign it will become a fixture in the zodiac. The personality changes will become permanent, and Ophiuchus will become vulnerable. Jalen, great power is at stake."

"How long is that?" Brennan asked, his voice a squeak. "Before earth passes . . ."

Gemini smoothed her hair. "Twenty-three hours."

Just under a day—about 8:30 tomorrow night. Earlier,

Gemini had said that Ophiuchus was with the one who needs healing. That had to be Nina, at the hospital. I calculated it quickly—she was about nine miles away. Nine miles in twenty-three hours. I could do this. I realized then that I had been pacing.

Was this all true? I had to defeat all twelve signs of the zodiac—including, apparently, our guide, Gemini—and find Ophiuchus? Nina always said, "Crazier things have happened!" But this was top-level crazy.

I looked back to see Ellie removing *The Keypers of the Zodiack* from her messenger bag. "It's this book!" she said. She chucked it into a nearby trash can. "I'll just dump it, and then we can go home. Right, Jalen? Home?"

Home. It did sound good.

"Hey, hey, hey!" the musician said. He jumped off the bench and ran to the garbage can. He dove into it headfirst. "You can't throw away a book!" His voice echoed inside the can.

He stood, the book in one hand, and shook a piece of lettuce from his long blond hair. "Someone will read—*hey!*" His gaze landed on Gemini. A slow grin spread across his tanned face like honey on peanut butter. "All right! A toga party! Where? Let's go! ToGA! ToGA! ToGA!"

Gemini walked up to the musician and plucked the book from his hand. "Thank you," she said, and whirled back to us. "The bus isn't coming. I think we should—"

"It's happening again, again, again. Again, again, again."

We heard the words coming from the shadows before we saw who said them. A disheveled man, dirty and crumpled, limped under the flickering streetlight. The buzzing lamp threw odd shadows down onto his face, shadows which looked like his face was morphing. Like the man we'd just battled, Taurus. The hairs on my arms stood up.

"It's happening again, again, again," he mumbled, pounding his ears with his fists, as if beating the demons out of his head. "Again, again, again . . ."

The musician's forehead wrinkled. "Hey, bud," he said softly, approaching this guy who was obviously a Keeper. The musician reached out his hand.

"Sir," Ellie said, a warning in her tone. "I wouldn't—"

But the musician waved her off, turned back to the disheveled man from the shadows. "Bud, you're right. The bus is sometimes late. Happens a lot. You need help getting somewhere?"

The closer the musician's hand got to this mumbling man, the wider the man's eyes grew, the louder and faster the murmuring became. "Againagainagain, againagainagain . . ."

The musician's fingertips lightly landed on the murmuring man's dusty coat. The man tossed his head back and howled like he'd been touched by a branding iron. My every muscle tightened, readying for what looked to be my next Challenge.

But the man twisted from beneath the musician's touch

and scurried up to me, locking eyes with me. He gripped both my arms, pinning them to my sides. I clenched my fists. "He is and she is," he mumbled through gray teeth, his breath stinking of rot. "He is and she is and he is and she is and . . ."

And the mumbling man scurried away, back into the shadows of the night. "He is and she is and he is and . . ."

Gemini huffed a sigh. "One last thing. As each Keeper surrenders, it will offer you a birthstone. You must chant, '*sic itur ad astra*'—'thus you shall go to the stars'—to cast them back to the heavens with their stone. Doing so ensures you've won the Challenge. Now. We really do need to get going. And it looks like we'll be on foot."

On foot. Suddenly that nine miles seemed so much farther away.

Do I continue?

I walked over to the bench and leaned my head against the cool plastic of the bus shelter. Through the clear roof, I could see the full moon, the stars. Massive ink-black splotches filled the sky. Empty voids where stars had once shone. The constellations of the zodiac—*missing*. It looked deep, dark, deadly, the clear nighttime sky with just a handful of stars.

I wished Nina were here to help me decide. Nina, once-brave Nina, who was now in terrible pain in her hospital bed. I thought of Nina giving up the fight, of giving in to the pain because she was a different person now.

Or my rock-solid mom, now crumbling apart, leaving to

go—where? I wished she could be here, tell me exactly what needed to be done and when, like the mom I loved.

I should be thankful, I supposed, that I had the help of two friends. And yet these two friends were now, for all purposes, strangers.

It's all so different. *Too* different.

Yes. I continue.

✳ ✳ ✳

I stood. "Let's go."

"Jalen!" A voice came at me.

I spun around.

The black Lincoln, the two men. The ones who had sliced the tip of my ear in two. The ones who thought we'd destroyed Brennan's truck. And they knew my name.

The musician snatched up his tuba. "Follow me!" he yelled. A quick look fired between Brennan, Ellie, and me. He seemed to know exactly what to do, so we followed.

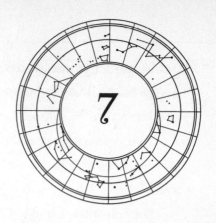

7

We ran over two blocks, up one, and the black car slid around every corner. With each pound of my feet, my brain thrummed: *They know my name.* With each pound of my feet, my ear throbbed. With each pound of my feet, I prayed they wouldn't lodge an arrow in my ribcage.

They had to be Keepers.

I thought it was my heart I heard pumping like mad, but it was that musician's tuba, *thump thump thump*, against his leg, the whole time we ran.

Brennan sprinted up beside the tuba player and jerked his head right. The musician nodded. Brennan took off between two houses, ducking under backyard play sets, jumping chain-link fences. The three of us followed him.

After fifteen minutes or so of running through other people's lives, we stopped. We'd lost the black car, we'd lost the whizzing arrows with their deadly points, but we had no idea where we were.

As we caught our breath, the musician pounded Brennan on the back. "Dude, you jump fences like a horse! Where'd you learn that?"

Brennan shrugged, and if it weren't night, I believe we'd have seen him blush. "Toilet-papering yards, I guess. Stupid stuff."

The tuba player nodded, then hunched again, resting his hands on his knees. He took longer than we did to catch his breath; he might've been in his late teens or early twenties. He looked up from his stoop, long blond bangs falling across his amber eyes. He shot us a brilliant white-toothed smile.

"Y'all in trouble or something?" he asked between pants.

"No," I answered.

"Yes," Ellie said.

I raised my eyebrows at her. The musician chuckled, then straightened. "Where's your friend? In the toga?"

Brennan pursed his lips. "I wouldn't exactly call her a friend," he mumbled.

The musician looked at each one of us, sizing us up. I felt for a moment like a piece of meat, being inspected, sniffed. But then he smiled, and his smile lit up the night. Dazzling. I couldn't help but grin back.

"I've done some stupid things, you know?" he said. The twinkle in his eye told me that, yes, troublemaking from this one was likely. Ellie nodded at him eagerly. Maybe *too* eagerly.

"Looks like y'all could use a hand. Where're you headed?"

"Nowhere," I said.

"Touro Infirmary," Ellie said.

I shot her a blazing look again. The musician chuckled again. "The hospital?"

I huffed and nodded. He stuck out his hand. He had calluses on his fingers, I assumed from punching tuba buttons. Daddy always said you could trust a man with calluses on his hand. I shook it. It was the perfect amount of handshake— not too tough, not too mealy. Just right.

"I'm Dillon," he said, flashing a grin. By the sound of her tiny gasp, I felt certain that Ellie, behind me, caught that grin of his. "I'm going to help you get to the hospital."

"Jalen," I said in return. I thought of the nine miles, the eleven Keepers between Nina and me. "I hope you do."

Brennan hadn't been watching our alliance form. "It's too dangerous," he said.

I withdrew my hand from the handshake. "What?"

"I said it's too dangerous, walking on the main roads," Brennan said. He turned around, his face creased with confusion. "If we can stay off roads altogether, that'd be best."

Ellie led us to a street sign and put the name of the road into her cell phone. "The river's just three blocks over. That way." She pointed into the night.

The banks of the Mississippi River were dark. They were

lined with a mix of neighborhoods and concrete, mud and docked barges. Walking along the river would take much longer; the curve of the Mississippi might add as much as a mile to our journey. But the Keepers chasing us in the car might rule out the river, because walking alongside it would take us so much longer than crossing over land. It didn't make much sense for us to go there. And so it was perfect.

✳ ✳ ✳

The next hour was relatively quiet: We were chased by a few snarly dogs, we glopped through patches of mud, Ellie tore her sweatshirt hood on a fence post. Dillon told her it made her look punk. Ellie grinned goofily, totally wiping out any traces of being "punk." Brennan and I rolled our eyes at each other.

It was easier sneaking through backyards than through industrial areas. The industrial parks glowed under fakey yellow streetlights. Many were surrounded with fences so high, it made me think they were carrying dangerous criminals on those barges, instead of barrels of oil and cages of seafood.

"Can we stop for a minute?" Dillon asked after about a mile. "I think I have a rock in my shoe." He started unlacing his black Converse hightop.

We were in a backyard, a friendly one with a swing set and dog toys scattered around. We had clamored through several yards whose signs had shouted, PRIVATE LAND—NO TRESPASSING at us before we'd trespassed. This yard had no signs and was welcoming by comparison. We waited for Dillon to tie his shoelaces.

The floodlights on the corner of the house flicked on, blinding us from above like searchlights.

"Oh, me! Are y'all all right?"

A woman stepped into the circle of light. She had to be a mom—she was very mom-like. Rather, I should say, like Every Mother—the mom stereotype. Right down to the pearl necklace, the apron, the perfectly coiffed hair, the lip-sticked smile. Until she took a deep drag off a cigarette.

"We're fine, thank you, ma'am," Brennan said. "Sorry to bother you."

The woman exhaled smoke from her nose. She flicked her cigarette into the grass and tapped out the glowing cinder with her shiny patent-leather pump. "No bother at all! Won't y'all come inside and call someone who can come pick y'all up? It's too late to be wandering around."

Y'all. She sounded like a native. "No thank you, ma'am," I said. "Sorry again."

But she'd already opened the door into her kitchen. Out wafted a warm cloud of heaven: soft yellow light flickering from the fireplace, the scent of baking chocolate chip cookies. I closed my eyes and inhaled long, cozy conversations with my Nina.

"Come on in, y'all," she drawled. "Y'all look like y'all could use a little mothering."

The way she said it made my heart twist. I *could* use a little mothering. My own mom had been so tough for so long. Soft cookies and soft firelight was exactly what I wanted right now.

"Okay," I said, drifting toward the shaft of warm light dancing from the kitchen.

And then, I saw her.

Nina.

She was inside by the fire, and she was holding out a cup of cocoa, just for me.

"Jalen," she said. "Come in."

I blinked. This was—*impossible*? How could she be better? How could she be *here*?

Maybe it was a miracle! This night had been full of strange things after all. *Crazier things have happened.* My heart sang. "Nina?" I breathed.

She nodded. "Come in."

The way she said it. It was too cold. Not full of honey and light at all. But my heart pulled me forward anyway. "You made cookies?" I asked.

"Sure, Jalen."

"Cookies?" Brennan grabbed my wrist. "I smell bacon!"

"Unh-uh, cinnamon," said Ellie, eyes closed.

Brennan stepped in front of me, grabbed my chin. "Jalen, it's a trick! Wake up, Jalen!"

"Hmmm?" I couldn't pull my eyes away from my Nina sitting at this table. All I wanted was to be inside next to the fire with her and her friend, that nice mama. I could do that, right?

"Jalen, we all smell something different! It's not your Nina. It's a trap! Wake up!"

"Mmmm." My feet moved through the soft grass. Just a few more steps and I'd be safe inside. Tucked away and warm at last.

"I'm sorry to do this, Jalen."

A *smack* sounded, and my cheek exploded in white-hot pain. My eyes shot open, orange daggers aimed at Brennan. "What the—"

"Let's go!" Brennan pulled me to the edge of the yard, out of the light and the cozy smells. But I had to pause at the edge of the yard once I heard the screaming.

Nina stood and upturned the kitchen table with a roar, scattering cookies and cocoa. "Cancer, you *idiot!*" she screamed. The mama person leaned against the house and struck a match off the brick.

Nina thrashed around inside the tiny home, smashing plates and cups. "I *told* you, we only needed to lure the one kid, not all three! You stingy, stingy thing. This is just like you, Cancer, trying to trap them all!"

The mama—Cancer—took a long drag off a new cigarette and exhaled, the smoke curling through the night sky like an acrid snake. Cancer flicked the lit match in Nina's direction. Nina's skin started bubbling and boiling. Mist rose off her flesh, making her look like an evaporating ghost. I reached out, but Brennan held me back. "Nina!" I shouted.

She turned and saw us still in the yard—Dillon sitting, jaw hanging open. Brennan gripping my elbow at the edge of the light. And Ellie, alone near the door.

Nina growled, her skin rearranging itself. She hunkered down and charged Ellie. Nina tackled her and they tumbled, rolling down a small grassy hill. Mist and stink masked them both.

"Nina?" I could only whisper. What happened? The mama ducked back in the house, clicked the lock shut, and turned off the spotlight, leaving us in the dark.

"Ellie!" Brennan shouted. He threw my elbow aside and charged into the mist. "Ellie?"

I charged in then, too. "Ellie!" My eyes stung from the mist, tears streaming down my cheeks. I couldn't see anything but green-gray, the fog was too thick, the night too dark. I started gagging. I heard Dillon's voice call in, "Hey! You guys okay?"

Then I heard it: Ellie's giggle. In stereo.

"Sure," Ellie said. Twice.

The fog lifted.

Two Ellies.

✳ ✳ ✳

My heart paused. I squeezed my eyes, opened them again, thinking this a trick of my watery sight. My Nina was now . . . Ellie? It couldn't be. My heart broke. Nina had been *right there*.

But no, I was seeing this correctly: two blond ponytails, two torn peace-sign sweatshirts, two messenger bags, two sets of nibbled fingernails.

"What the——?" Brennan choked.

"Whoa," Dillon breathed.

Ellie One turned to Ellie Two. (Or maybe it was Ellie Two who turned to Ellie One?) Then the other Ellie turned as well. The Ellies looked at one another.

And both screamed.

Both started crying.

"Wait, wait, wait," I said. I grabbed each Ellie by the shoulder. Both felt real, both sets of eyes were so *human*. No trace of my Nina left. No trace. I gripped the Ellies harder, looking from one Ellie to the other, my heart thudding in my ears. Exact mirror images. Identical. Twins.

"Twins," Brennan muttered. "Gemini——the twins."

"But where is *our* Gemini?" I scanned the area in desperation, hoping for a glimpse of a billowing toga. What was going on? "Is this her?" I remembered the warning Gemini had given back at my house, the warning she'd issued *before* helping us: *I won't be so polite the next time our paths cross.* Had she just been tricking us, being nice until now?

"Jalen, it's me! I'm Ellie! I'm her!" one of the Ellies claimed.

"Jalen, no! It's me! She's not—she's . . ." More tears.

"Jalen, you have to believe me!" Red-faced anger from this Ellie.

"Jalen, don't! It's me! Don't you believe me?"

I swallowed hard. I didn't know which Ellie was *my* Ellie. Was I supposed to guess? I blinked back tears. If this had happened hours ago, I'd know my Ellie without a doubt. But the new Ellie . . . could I pick her out for certain?

"Who is your homeroom teacher?" I choked out.

"Mrs. McGill," they answered like a chorus. They turned to each other and grew teary-eyed again.

"What did you dress as for Halloween last year?" Brennan asked.

Both Ellies answered in unison, "A hippie." One Ellie started shaking, the other bit her lip and tried to reel in the tears.

"Whoa," Dillon said again. His wide eyes glowed in the night like a cat's.

The book! Real Ellie had a copy of *The Keypers of the Zodiack*.

"Let me see the book," I said.

Both Ellies reached into the messenger bag strapped across her chest and retrieved identical copies of *The Keypers of the Zodiack*. Great. Now there were *two* copies of this dangerous book. I flipped through both in panic. Identical, as far as I could tell. I turned to the entry on Gemini and read.

> " 'Gemini, the twins. June 20–July 20. Thou art charming times two, Gemini. Thine impulsive, curious nature provides thee with a cache of friends, albeit none too dear—thy cynicism and impatience makes deep relationships rare. Thou couldst not risk another coming between thee and thy twin. But, this same trait allows thee an adaptability unseen in others. Thou art a quick-witted, restless communicator, sometimes breathing life into gatherings, sometimes driving others to madness. Remember, Gemini, that thy duality oft leads to deception. In the end, thou canst not abide suffering, and thou will make great sacrifices to avoid seeing loved ones destruct.' "

By now, one Ellie was sobbing to the point of gagging. The other sat on the curb, holding her head and muttering, "No, no, no!"

Which was *Ellie*? I shook my head and turned to Brennan.

"Brennan, do you—?"

He trembled. He paced between the two, looking each squarely in the eyes. He trembled more. "No."

More wails from both Ellies this time.

At last, Gemini, our guide, appeared. Dillon scrambled backward in the dirt.

"What is this?" I flung my hand at these two versions of my best friend. "Is this a Gemini twin? Why doesn't she look like you? Where did Nina go?"

Gemini took a shaky breath and stroked her hair. "I warned that you would face all twelve Keepers, and this is your Gemini Challenge, Jalen. The Gemini power is the power to twin anyone in the world, living or dead. You must pick which is your best friend and defeat the other."

"Defeat?" I wailed. I looked at both Ellies, both looking at me with tear-stained faces and red-rimmed, pleading eyes. Gemini's twin—obviously the *evil* twin—had mimicked Nina to trap me. And now? "What does that mean, defeat?"

"I believe you know what it means," Gemini whispered to the ground. "Consider this. It's better than having to battle your grandmother."

Fire choked me. I growled, balled my fist, and punched the brick house. My knuckles exploded in pain.

Brennan ran at our guide in a tackle stance. "Give me back my *sister*!" But before he even touched her, he flew backward, like he had bounced off a wall.

"Ah, ah, ah!" our guide said, twitching her finger. Her midnight eyes throbbed, darker than anything else in the night. "Think about your actions. You do not need to anger me."

I grabbed one Ellie's hand, paused, then grabbed the other Ellie's hand, too. One of my hands touched my best friend. The other one touched a predator. Which was which?

"You're both coming."

8

Running away from that cozy spot was like getting a bucket of ice water dumped over my head. Alarming, awful, but awakening. No Nina, an extra Ellie. We stopped at last to catch our breath.

I was surprised Dillon stuck by us. "You're still here," I said between breaths. He nodded and dropped his tuba, a wheeze sounding under his panting.

"Y'all are obviously in some deep doo-doo," he said, lifting his chin at the pair of Ellies. "I'm not leaving you. It's just getting interesting." He winked at me. Sparks glimmered inside my chest when he did, despite where we were.

The area was industrial, dark, with one solitary barge docked on the river. The river *slap-slap-slapped* the barge, the bank. A crane on bulldozer wheels hoisted an empty seafood cage above the barge. Tomorrow the crane would lower the huge cage, and the barge would bring it back to the fishing boats in the Gulf. Life moving forward, despite everyone changing. It would, right? Move forward?

"So what's going on here, exactly?" Dillon asked. "If I'm going to help you, I want to know what we're up against." We paused, and then I nodded at Brennan. He started to explain, telling Dillon all about the Keepers of the Zodiac with huge arm gestures and oversize, snarling facial expressions. This was where Dillon would leave us for sure. And probably call the police. And probably a few psychiatrists.

I had to turn away from Brennan's explanation, because I hardly believed it myself. I looked instead from one Ellie to the other. I felt nothing. Nada. Before, I had been excellent at reading people. No, if I'm being honest, let's call it what it was: *judging people*. But now—nothing. One of the Ellies saw my eyes darting between her and her twin, and a tear slid down her cheek. Wouldn't *that* be the real Ellie? Could the Keepers be *that* accurate? And yet I'd seen people transform into beasts just this evening. They'd almost fooled me, trapping me by impersonating my own Nina. Surely an imposter Ellie could whip up a few tears on command. No, I couldn't just *guess*. The danger of guessing wrong was too great. I had to be certain.

"So then who was that?" Dillon asked.

I startled at his question.

Dillon licked his lips, and it made me realize how thirsty I was. "I mean, not the crazy old lady turning young." He looked at the pair of Ellies. "No offense. I mean that mom?"

Both Ellies dug *The Keypers of the Zodiack* from a messenger bag, like it was a race to see who could get the answer the fastest. "Cancer!" they both shouted.

They started reading in a blur of words:

" 'Cancer, the crab. July 21–August 9.' "

"Stop!" I snapped. Both Ellie heads shot up. My knee bounced—still no clue which twin was which. I cracked my knuckles. "I can't understand when you both read." I pointed at the closest Ellie.

"You," I said. "Read." The other Ellie slammed her copy of the book closed and kicked the gravel. The closest Ellie gloated and read like the teacher's pet.

" 'Cancer, the crab. July 21–August 9. Cancer, thou wert sent by King Eurystheus to distract Hercules while he battled the nine-headed Hydra sea monster. That is therefore thy gift: the gift of distraction. Thou preferest to think of it as the gift of hospitality. Though it comes not without a price: One must praise thine efforts in order to gain thine affections. But when thine affections are won, no one is more nurturing or caring than thou art. Thy need for constant love and encouragement contradicts thy lack of trust in others. Contradiction, in fact, is at thy core. Thy moods are shifty and unpredictable, from sullen to smiling to stormy in seconds. Cancer, thou art a feeling being, ruled by the heart. And yet thy memory is long, and when thou feelest wronged, thy need to bury thine opponents overwhelms. Avoid this need, as it may disrupt sought-after* *security. The pressure thou placest upon thyself is too intense; beware lest thou explode."*

"Well, that doesn't paint a pretty picture at all, does it?"

I spun to see Cancer standing there, a jacket thrust out to me. A cigarette ember bounced an inch from her red lips. The irony of the fact that Cancer was a smoker was not lost on me. "Mmm-hmmm," she breathed. "Not pretty at all."

Smoke filtered out of her nostrils. I was reminded of a dragon. A dragon in an apron.

"Jalen," she breathed in a cloud of smoke. "At least, put on this jacket. You look so cold."

Cold. I was cold. Wasn't I?

"No!" I said. I grit my teeth to prevent them from suddenly chattering. I *wasn't* cold. Why did I want that jacket so badly? "No, not cold."

Cancer lowered the jacket, stomped out her glowing cigarette. The orange fire squashed so quickly beneath her pointy patent-leather toe. "No jacket then. Fine."

Cancer's lipsticked smile stretched as tight as a rubber band across her face, but her eyes were steely knives. The picture of contradiction. Her maternal leanings tugged her in one direction, her fury and power and madness pulled her in the other. Cancer had a hard shell and a mighty pinch.

I longed for that jacket. It looked cozy and warm and soft. It would protect me.

"No jacket," she said, her words etched like ice on air. "Be cold."

"And *you,*" she said, spinning and pointing at one of the Ellies. "I'll show you who's an idiot."

And then, she disintegrated. Cancer dissolved like candle wax, melting into a low pool of smelly mist. The apron strings untied and shriveled into long, pinching claws. The lipstick swelled and spread across her skin, turning every inch of her red. The pearl necklace hardened into a tough outer shell. Cancer doubled into two crabs, then again to four, then again and again and again.

I scurried backward, but Ellie—the one nearby, the one she had called an idiot—stumbled and fell. A tidal wave of slick crabs swelled from the mist, higher and higher and higher, a writhing, crawling wave of crustaceans. It crashed down over a screaming Ellie.

"Ellie!" I yelled too late.

A shrill creak split the air, the sound of rusted metal forced into action. The bulldozer crane behind me whirled about. The seafood cage was no longer empty; it was teeming with hundreds of crusty, snapping crabs.

The hatch on the cage sprang open, and hundreds of crabs rained down on top of the existing pile. It buried Ellie under another wave of crab bodies, crab legs, crab claws.

It was a small mountain of crustaceans, taller and wider than a bus, and it had swallowed one of the Ellies whole. We had to dig her out of there. She wouldn't be able to breathe for long under those pounds and pounds of crabs. But digging through a pile of crabs was like digging through a pile of sharp slabs of rock, plus slime and stink.

Brennan and Dillon had already started flinging clumps of crab bodies aside. I did the same. The other Ellie, the free Ellie, grabbed my elbow.

"Jalen, stop! I'm the real Ellie! Stop digging—you're saving a Keeper!"

I paused and looked into her green eyes. They twinkled—with what? Tears? Amusement?

"Jalen, that is Gemini under there. You heard what Cancer said! She's getting even with Gemini for calling her an idiot! Let them duke it out!" Ellie grabbed me by the elbow and started pulling me away. I followed.

But. Wasn't she pulling a little too hard?

Was this Ellie telling the truth? Or was this a Keeper, trying to convince me to stop rescuing my best friend? That would weaken me more than anything else the Keepers could conjure if I was somehow involved in hurting my friends. They'd defeat me for certain if that happened.

"Jalen!" Brennan yelled over the clicking crabs. "Where are you going?"

It could be a trick, couldn't it? Cancer could be tricking me. She would trick me into thinking she was just getting even with Gemini, when it was actually *my* Ellie under there.

Cancer was manipulative. She would do that, wouldn't she? To win?

"Don't you believe me, Jalen?" this Ellie asked. Her voice wavered.

If I didn't dig for the buried Ellie, I was choosing, wasn't I? Which Ellie I thought was mine? I wasn't ready to make that choice.

"I can't," I said. And I didn't have any more time to ponder which Ellie was which. I decided to climb.

But climbing a hill of clicking, shifty crab bodies wasn't easy. Placing my feet and hands on them did relatively nothing; the crabs I touched would simply slide down the mountain of shell to the bottom, tiny landslides every time I tried to gain traction. And crabs are made of everything awful: hard shells, thick pinchers, slick bodies, heavy stink. The cut on my ear stung like acid from all the crab muck.

My hands would plunge into the swarm and I'd feel a sharp pinch. I'd remove my hand to find a crab clamped onto my finger, and I'd have to sling it aside before starting again. I could only imagine what Ellie was going through in there at the heart of the crab hive. I couldn't even hear if she was screaming; the click-clacking of hundreds of crab legs and pinchers was near deafening. And the other Ellie, the free one, kept begging me, begging Brennan, begging Dillon, to believe that she was *our* Ellie. It was hard not to believe her.

I finally decided to keep my feet planted on the ground. I started flinging the crabs aside with my hands, like a dog digging a hole. It was faster, yes, but the crabs I launched to either side marched back to their pack like an army of zombies.

I plunged my hand into the mass again and drew it back sharply—a sliver of crab shell pierced me under my fingernail. I saw white, then orange anger cleared the pain. My anger was sharper than these crabs. I knew this.

That's when I saw Brennan scaling the bulldozer. Free Ellie pleaded with him to get down, begged him to believe her. He ignored her. He stood on top of the six-foot-high treaded wheels, covered his face with his arms, and jumped into the clot.

"Brennan, wait!" I yelled. He disappeared almost immediately. Between seeing that and the overpowering stench of the crabs, I turned my head to the side and retched. The free Ellie sobbed and shouted, "No!" She plunged her hands in at last, covering herself in slime.

Would a Keeper do that? I wondered. Appear so concerned about Brennan? I decided that, yes, she would if she's playing the game right. If I lose the Gemini Challenge by guessing the incorrect Ellie, then she's doing everything in her power to confuse me. I slicked back my hair with my forearm, leaving a trail of gooey crab chunks across my scalp. I kept digging.

Moments later, the other Ellie's head shot out of the

center of the fester like she was propelled from below. She gulped in a deep, wheezing breath. Brennan's head popped up next to hers, and then the side of the mountain began to crumble. Brennan had righted Ellie on her feet. They were pushing their way through the crabs.

Dillon grabbed them both and dragged them aside, the crab muck shimmering on them all. Ellie had crabs tangled in her hair and a deep gash on her left cheek. She wasn't screaming, but tears streamed down her face, cleaning away blood and crab guts. Brennan yanked a crab pinched to his ear and howled.

Cancer wasn't done with us yet. The crabs thinned out and scurried around us, turning the ground into a moving, swelling thing.

Brennan stepped on a crab and slipped. When he stood again, a dozen crabs were pinched to his skin. He looked down, and at that moment, I saw his eyes twinkle.

He'd crushed one of them! Cancer's horoscope came barreling back to me: *The pressure thou placest upon thyself is too intense.* We began stomping and crushing crabs as quickly as we could to defeat them, to find that cursed birthstone. Dillon was a champion crab crusher. But squashing crabs is difficult; it takes far more force than simply stomping a cockroach. And it was slippery work. Each of us fell several times, and each time we got up, we had dozens of pinchers embedded in our skin.

One of the Ellies had managed to climb on top of a small metal electrical transformer. Although the crabs couldn't climb the slick metal box, they had figured out that if they stacked one upon the other, they could reach their prey eventually.

There were too many crabs, and we were tired. I whipped around, trying to hop on one of the larger crabs in my vicinity, when the bulldozer again caught my eye.

Please let the keys be in it, I thought. Then, *Please let bulldozers even have keys.* I ran, I slipped, I skidded the dozen or so yards to the bulldozer and climbed aboard.

Maybe someone up there heard my prayer because the keys dangled in the bulldozer's ignition. I cranked the engine, and the bulldozer snapped forward like a dinosaur awakened.

I soon figured out that the lever in the floor was how to steer the thing, like a joystick in a video game. The dozer lurched herky-jerky forward, left, right, slinging me around in its metal cab, swaying the crane, swinging the seafood cage like a wrecking ball.

But it was working! The crabs popped like pimples under the weight of the bulldozer's tread. I crunched as many as I could and scanned the dark area for my friends.

Brennan, Dillon, and the other Ellie had joined Ellie One on top of the transformer. The two Ellies clawed at each other like one would surely push the other off into the nest of crabs. And the crabs were almost high enough to reach them. I steered the bulldozer as best I could toward the box.

Brennan looked at the rapidly approaching bulldozer with wide eyes. I leaned out of the cab and yelled, "Jump! On one!" I held up three fingers as high as I could outside the cab in case he hadn't heard me. *Oh, please—let him have heard me.*

Brennan saw my fingers and nodded.

"Three!" I yelled. Three fingers. The bulldozer ground forward, crushing crabs, swinging the crane hook behind me.

"Two!" Two fingers. Mere feet away from my best friends. They were now not only timing the approach of the bulldozer but were also swatting away the crabs that had managed to stack up high enough to attack their feet and legs.

"ONE!" One finger. Brennan and Dillon and Ellie and Ellie hurled themselves to my left, and the bulldozer plowed into the transformer, which was now festering with crabs. The transformer cracked open and sparks of electricity sizzled and spit. Crab parts flew everywhere, and every light for as far as we could see went out.

Beware lest thou explode.

The bulldozer was pushed back by the force of the impact, but the electrical box had been too small to cause such a massive machine much harm. I couldn't say the same for the crabs, however. They were electrocuted, their tiny crab parts twitching with shock.

I climbed out of the cab. "Ellie? Brennan? Dillon?"

I heard their voices in the dark night, a night even darker now. "We're here."

I choked on a sob and ran to the sound of their voices. We hugged as a group for a minute, both Ellies panting and sobbing, both with gashes on their cheeks, glop in their hair. Dillon pulled away.

"You guys stink," he said with a grin.

We all breathed out. We did stink. We were slimy and wet and covered in muck and a little blood. I looked around. "How in the world are we going to find the birthstone in the dark?"

One of the Ellies wiped a chunk of crab goo off her face and flung it aside. She pulled the birthstone, a ripe red ruby, out of her sweatshirt pocket.

"You're welcome," she said. She glared at the other Ellie.

I held the birthstone aloft and said my chant, *"Sic itur ad astra."* If I hadn't just been attacked by these creatures and then blown them to bits, I'd have thought that the sparkling trails skittering into the skies were what took my breath away.

Two Keepers down, ten to go.

And there we stood, watching Cancer ascend into the

heavens, reforming into a crab constellation, when a click sounded behind us.

I jumped and whirled around, terrified that we'd missed a crab. A flashlight beam blinded me.

"There you are, Jalen Jones. I think you better come with us."

9

The men from the car," an Ellie whispered.

The men with the arrows, I thought. The tip of my ear throbbed.

"Jalen Jones." The second man stepped forward into the edge of the light.

"Can I help you?" I asked, squinting at him. I felt one eyebrow arch up, punctuating the question. Cool! I'd always wanted to be able to do that. Now, apparently I could.

He extended a huge hand, handshake-style. I didn't shake it.

"I'm Agent Cygnus. And this—" he shoved his partner with his elbow, causing the flashlight beam to lower at last. "This is Agent Griffin. I hope we didn't scare you three too badly? Griffin here has been sneaking around like a spy on steroids ever since the personality shift. Stupid rookie."

My eyes adjusted back to the night. I couldn't decide if the red spots I saw were from the blinding light or the blinding anger. But I'd caught one thing he'd said: "you *three*"?

I stole a sideways glance. Dillon had snuck away. Over the shoulder of the guy with the flashlight, he signaled me, jumping and waving. *Shhhhh,* he gestured, finger over lips. I tried not to nod at him; he was obviously up to something, and I didn't want these guys to see. But still—*three*?

This guy couldn't see the other Ellie! Then, suddenly, I realized—neither could I. The other Ellie, the second Ellie—gone. Disappeared, like Gemini.

If Ellie Part Deux was gone, these people *had* to be human. It was too risky for her to stay around humans who hadn't touched the book; we'd easily discover which was Fake Ellie and which was Real Ellie based on who was overlooked. I practically tackled my Ellie, I hugged her so hard. As I did, she whispered into my hair.

"Jalen. They know something about a personality shift."

They do? Yes—they do! The agent. He'd said, *"Ever since the personality shift."*

Hope glowed inside me. Others—other *humans,* apparently—knew about the shift.

How *much* did they know? Did they know I'd caused it? Would I be in a world of trouble? Based on the looks of these men and the fact that they'd launched arrows at my back, my best guess was that they knew quite a lot.

But they said they were agents. FBI? They might be able to help us. Maybe they could even take us to Nina!

Agent Cygnus had been rambling on about protocol

when approaching a suspect and that Agent Griffin was obviously not following said protocol and, hey, what do you expect from a rookie and well-gosh-sorry. He crossed to the car and opened the back door. "Come with us, Jalen. You look like you could use a hot shower and a warm meal."

My stomach rumbled, placing its vote.

Ellie grabbed my hand and shook her head. The events of the night had left her distrustful. And I had to agree—the slice in my ear hadn't just appeared there.

Ziiiiip! I flinched. As if my thoughts had made it happen, an arrow zippered by me and planted itself in the ground just in front of Agent Cygnus, the staff waggling. *Ziiiiip!* Another, just in front of Agent Griffin. The sound of those arrows slicing the air so cleanly made me shiver, but neither agent recoiled. The warm smile never left Agent Cygnus's face.

They obviously couldn't *see* the arrows. Who had fired them before?

Sagittarius. The archer. And my former sign.

I took a step forward, fearing that another arrow might slice open our skin at any moment. We had to get out of here. Into the car—that'd be safe. "Okay," I said. "Let's—"

But the bulldozer engine roared to life, drowning out the rest of my sentence. I turned to see Dillon steering the dozer straight for the agents' car.

Agent Griffin ran at the thing, leaving a wave of curse

words in his wake. The bulldozer plowed straight toward him.

That was enough for Ellie; she took off running along the dark riverbank. Brennan and I exchanged a glance before we followed.

As the night swallowed us, we heard the bulldozer crush the car.

✳ ✳ ✳

After running for eight or nine blocks, we paused at an intersection. There was light here, but we chose to catch our breath in the shadows. I felt bad—we'd left Dillon behind. Had they caught him? Or had he escaped? Would he catch up to us? Nah, surely not. Surely, he'd bail. I know I would. We'd have to keep going without him. Our time was ticking away.

I finally sucked enough air into my lungs to look up from the tips of my tennis shoes—

—and there were two Ellies.

"No!" I yelled. "No, no, no!" Why hadn't I held on to Ellie's hand? Watched with eagle eyes for the other Ellie to reappear? I spun and kicked the brick wall behind me. Stupid. Now my toes hurt, too. One of the Ellies looked positively sick at seeing her twin, her skin paling under the crusty blood on her cheek, compliments of Cancer. The other just bit her lip while silent tears mixed with her cut. One of these two was an excellent actress. Which one?

Gemini, our guide, was there now. She handed each Ellie a scrap of cloth, telling each to hold it to the cut on her face.

"How did they find us?" an Ellie asked, dabbing her cheek.

Brennan plucked the cell phone out of one of the Ellie's back jeans pocket and held it up. The screen showed seven new texts from Ellie's mom.

"You don't even have to make a call, you know," Brennan said. "It just has to be on." He tossed it onto the sidewalk and raised his foot, ready to crush it.

"Wait!" I yelled. "I want to try my mom again first."

I called. It rang and rang and rang and went to voice mail. Finally on my fourth try, my mom's wailing ripped through the phone.

"Jalen?" she said through sobs.

The fist around my heart clenched harder. "Mom, where are you? I've been trying to—"

"Jalen, honey, I'm sorry, but I can't stay. I can't. Where's your father? Where *is* he?"

"Dad? What are you talking about? Mom, you have to stay! Please stay with Nina! Where are you?"

My mom retched from all the crying. "N-Nina?" she said at last.

"Aren't you with her? Mom!"

"Jalen," my mom choked out. "I have to find him."

The line went dead.

＊ ＊ ＊

I knew it. I knew Mom always believed Dad's disappearance meant that he walked out on us, left when I got so very sick. She had never believed he was dead. And now she was planning on trying to find him?

Did her personality shift make her want to search for him, instead of shutting him out?

And then, for the first time since I was nine years old, I wondered, Is *he still alive?* Could *he have just . . . left?*

"No!" I yelled. I smashed the phone down on the sidewalk, but instead of shattering into satisfying pieces, it bounced and skidded against one of the Ellie's sneakers.

She stooped and picked it up. "That won't help us at all."

She pulled a matching cell phone out of her pocket. Of course—two cells. Twice as dangerous. She pointed to a taxi sitting at the red light in the intersection.

"You walk in the crosswalk, in front of the taxi," she told us. Brennan looked at me and shrugged.

I took a shaky breath but nodded. We crossed—Brennan, Gemini, the other Ellie, and me. As we did, the Ellie with the phones cut behind the taxi and discreetly tucked both cell phones in the gap between the back window and the trunk.

The light turned green. The taxi took off with both phones, heading in the direction opposite ours.

"What are you *doing*?" the other Ellie shrieked.

I watched as contact with my mom rolled away. My stomach knotted.

I spit through gritted teeth, "I don't think my *friend* would do that."

"I was just trying to help," Ellie said, her voice wavering. Then her eyes narrowed. "Are you saying I'm a Keeper, Jalen? Do you really want to make that kind of accusation?"

The shadows in her statement tamped down my anger a notch. *Was* I certain? Our cell phones rolling far away from us *was* a good idea. Could it be Real Ellie, trying to help?

I sighed. "We needed those phones."

"Yes! We did!" the other Ellie shrieked.

"For what?" Ellie asked. "So those agents could hunt us down?"

"We might've been able to trust them, you know," I said.

Ellie placed her hands on her hips. "No, I don't know. Those guys could be lions or scorpions or some other kind of awful creatures. I only know I can trust the two of you." She glared at Gemini, at the other Ellie, and whipped around. She headed what I guessed was west, toward Algiers.

I glanced at Gemini. If she knew which Ellie was real and which was fake, she was offering no hints. Which one *was* it, walking away?

If it was my friend, if it truly was . . . well, then, my heart ached for her. Scared, distrustful Ellie. I remember how lonely distrust feels. I should—it was only hours before that I was steeped in it.

We followed the stomping Ellie for a block or two before Brennan said with a wrinkled forehead, "Hey, is this the right way? Without those phones, we don't know where we're headed." I wished Dillon was still with us. He'd know what to do.

The Ellie closest to us stopped. She pointed at a tiny convenience store ahead, the only business open on this side of the river at this time of night. "Ever hear of a map, guys?"

I gritted my teeth.

The neon signs in the window threw red and blue and yellow light onto the sidewalk. I swung open the door. A buzzer screeched with our entrance. The teen behind the counter didn't even look up. I doubted he heard us over the punk music blasting through his earbuds.

Maps of New Orleans were up front, stuffed into a teetering circular metal rack with postcards and snow globes of the city—like it ever snowed in New Orleans. Brennan looked at a few maps and picked one.

At the counter, one of the Ellies leaned over the clear glass and pointed at a lottery ticket.

"Hey!" she shouted to the guy. His eyes opened just a slit.

"We want one of those!" She jabbed her finger at the case. "And this." She took the map from Brennan and placed it on the counter.

My heart sped up. She was buying a lottery ticket? We weren't eighteen. I'd never done something like that before. Surely, we'd never get away with it. But it reminded me about the hospital rules and the mom rules and all the rules. Forget the rules—forget them! Maybe *this* was the Ellie who had insisted we take *The Keypers of the Zodiack* out of Madame Beausoleil's shop.

The teen behind the counter whipped his dyed-black bangs out of his eyes, pushed up the sleeves on his red plaid shirt, and ripped off a ticket. He tossed it on the counter, closed his eyes, and resumed bobbing his head to the music. Ellie slid the money to him, but he didn't even pick it up.

"Here." She held the ticket out to me. Was she smirking or smiling? "Let's test our luck."

The lottery ticket said, "Your Lucky Stars: 12 Chances to Win!" Twelve scratch-off patches were arranged in a circle on a zodiac calendar, Aries through Pisces.

"Ellie!" Brennan whispered. "You bought a lotto ticket?"

But I was already scratching off the gray gunk with my thumbnail. I started at the top with Aries and worked my way through each sign, just knowing I'd see a "You Win!" under one of the patches.

Under each patch was a "No." And not just a "No," but a

rejection unique to that sign, from Aries, "Yeah, right." To Libra, "Try again!" To Leo, "Nope." To Pisces, "Better Luck Next Time!"

"I lost." My hands grew clammy. This twelve-sign zodiac calendar taunted me, teased me, predicted *me* the loser.

Somehow, I still had a hard time believing that horoscopes could define me, could predict my actions and reactions. That these Keepers could pull a string and I would bow like a puppet. Don't I have some sort of say in the matter?

I tore the lottery ticket into tiny, fierce pieces and threw them on the floor. I stormed out, clutching the map.

Outside, I breathed in cool air, trying to control some of this orange anger. It was harder to do than I ever imagined. I shook, I was so angry. Brennan laid a gentle hand on my elbow, but I shrugged it off. And great—guilt now, too.

The door buzzer screamed into the cool night air. The convenience store clerk came out and plucked an earbud from one of his ears. "Hey!" he shouted.

Rats. He knew we weren't eighteen. Or he was ticked that I threw that torn-up ticket all over the floor. So this is what it felt like to forget the rules.

"Hey, sorry—" I started. But he collapsed, melting into the shadows beneath the neon-splattered sidewalk. In the blue-green light, I watched the wires of his headphones stretch and thicken and curl, turning into yellowish horns. His plaid shirt grew shaggy, morphing into coarse spotted fur. Before I could even turn to run, a small goat galloped from the rotten mist and head-butted me in the gut.

Oof! I dropped the map. The goat slurped it up with a disgustingly long pink tongue. He chewed once, gulped, then turned and trotted into invisibility. It obviously wasn't time for my Challenge with this Keeper yet.

"See you later, Capricorn," I uttered, clutching my stomach.

"Let's just get another—" Brennan turned toward the store but stopped.

The convenience store was gone. A shadowy, boarded-up building with bars on the windows stood there instead.

✳ ✳ ✳

One of the Ellies marched away, and we followed. Like a whisper, Gemini was beside me. When I saw her, I honestly couldn't remember if she'd been walking with us the whole time or not.

"Why don't you stay with us?" I asked.

She pulled her manicured fingernails through her hair. "It's better if the others don't know I'm helping you. They . . . wouldn't be pleased." She paused. "Do you want me here?"

The question surprised me, but the sharpness of my answer surprised me even more: "All I want is to get to my Nina."

Gemini nodded. "You've lost someone before."

Warmth flashed through me. *Had* I lost him? Or had he left? Lost or left?

My dad's fishing boat had been found empty off the Cameron Jetty. The boat itself was fine, like it had just run ashore. But my dad, an excellent fisherman and boater, had vanished. They dredged the bottom of the sea with a huge ugly claw for a week. Nothing rose but sand and mud. Nothing.

Right after he disappeared, I played the *lost or left* game for months. Nina finally convinced me, without a doubt, that we'd lost him. Now, though, I wasn't so sure.

Whoever said that loss gets easier with time was a liar. Here's what really happens: The spaces between the times you miss them grow longer. Then, when you do remember to miss them again, it's still with a stabbing pain to the heart. And you have guilt. Guilt because it's been too long since you missed them last.

Gemini put her hand on my shoulder. Surprisingly, I didn't shirk from it.

"Those wounds take a long time to heal."

I cracked my knuckles. Yes, they did, and I didn't want to reopen them now.

For blocks and blocks, we followed Ellie in silence. Was everyone else wondering which sign we'd meet up with next? Wondering how we'd defeat them? Wondering if we'd ever get back to "normal"? Wondering how we got here?

Here. I blinked at the bulldozer crane under the orangey yellow light in the distance. Were we——?

"No," Brennan breathed. Then he sprinted forward and pushed what might be his sister from behind. "We're back at the bulldozer! You led us the wrong way!"

I grabbed the Ellie who had been leading us by the wrist. My eyes darted between her and the other Ellie, who stood away from our group, blinking through tears.

"You led us backwards," I whispered. "Ellie—my *friend* Ellie—wouldn't sabotage me like this."

The Ellie whose wrist I held started to tremble. "Jalen," she whispered. "Let's just go home, okay? Home? I'm scared, and I don't want to do this anymore."

I looked over at the other Ellie. "She's lying, Jalen. Don't listen to her. I want to help you."

"I'm not lying," this Ellie squeaked. She shook so hard her messenger bag slipped off her shoulder. "I'm not."

I closed my eyes and my head fell back. When I opened my eyes again, I was looking into the dark night sky. A few more stars were visible now. My victories, twinkling down from above.

I wasn't certain, still. I sighed to prevent exploding and released Ellie's wrist. "Okay, where are we? How do we get to Algiers?"

The street signs told me nothing. I looked to Brennan. "Algiers?"

Brennan's head snapped from landmark to landmark, like he was trying desperately to find something, anything that would tell him which direction we should go. The river. Before, he'd always used the river as his compass.

Now, he bit his lip and looked at me with wild eyes. "I don't know."

It was the first time I'd seen a true weakness in After Brennan. I didn't like it.

✳ ✳ ✳

We were still standing there, trying to figure out east from west when a familiar voice whispered from the shadows, "You came back!"

Dillon! I smiled at the thought of him. But I frowned at the sight of him. He stumbled into the light with a limp.

Oh, no! Why didn't I insist we come back for him? Why? Because of some stupid deadline, that's why.

The Ellies glommed onto to him, cooing and petting him. "Dillon, are you okay?" "Where does it hurt, Dillon? Where?"

But Dillon just chuckled. "Hey, I'm alright. Just a sprained ankle. Got it trying to make some heroic leap out of that dozer. But what are y'all doing here? You got a deadline to meet!"

I shook my head. "Forget that," I said. "Are you sure you're alright?"

Gemini took a look at his puffy ankle. She tore a strip of fabric off the hem of her toga with her teeth and wrapped it.

"I'm fine, I'm fine," he said with a wince. "Didn't even use up one of my nine lives." He tossed back his head and laughed so boisterously, we couldn't help but join in. "Well, what are we waiting for?" said a newly bandaged Dillon. He snatched up his tuba with a grin and started limping away. "Follow me."

10

We walked for hours and miles, hours and miles, the dried crab on our skin crusty and itchy, the dried crab on our clothes stinky and crunchy. Every noise in the night made us jump. Around every corner, something lurked, waiting in attack mode. We were sure of it. It made a long walk longer.

And my feet were dragging. Not because I was tired, not really. I was—for the first time since we started this journey—unsure. Dillon had been hurt. And that stupid lottery ticket deeming me a loser. What had I *done*, unlocking that lock? And worse, it didn't appear that I could do anything to undo it. Except keep going.

When we arrived at the ferry at Algiers Point, the sun was peeking over the horizon, a tangerine sun warming the sky in shades of pink and purple and gray. The bells of Saint Louis Cathedral across the river chimed six o'clock.

Six o'clock. We'd only traveled about two and a half

miles since last night. We still had another six or seven to go before 8:30 tonight. And still ten Keepers to defeat.

The ferry ran every fifteen minutes, and one was not docked at the station yet. Brennan and I sat on a concrete bench in the ferry station and looked out over the expanse of the muddy Mississippi River. Gemini insisted on looking at Dillon's ankle, at both Ellies' cuts. I studied her again. Did she know which Ellie was my Ellie? If so, she was doing an excellent job of hiding it.

My toes tapped, waiting on that darned ferry, but we'd have to cross the river by boat. My toes bouncing on the metal floor seemed to ask, *Lost or left? Lost or left?* The question I hadn't asked about my dad since I was nine was back. Yet another thing I'd unlocked: insecurities about my dad. Super.

Was I nervous to get on this boat? Was that it? I couldn't tell. I hoped not. We didn't have time to make it to the Crescent City Connection Bridge.

Brennan placed his hand on my knee to stop it from bouncing. Had he heard my feet tapping out those silly questions, too? He smiled, and a new kind of warmth flushed my skin.

Brennan had once been a friend. Well, he'd been nice— my best friend's nice older brother. But then my dad's accident happened, and Brennan faded into the background. That was okay—a lot of people didn't know what to say to me. But when he finally started paying attention to me again, it had been an insult here, a jab there. Remembering it now, I jerked my knee away from his hand.

His forehead wrinkled. "Things were really different before, huh? And you remember it?"

I nodded at the pavement.

I heard him swallow. "Was I—you know? A good person?"

I sniffled, then felt hot. "Yeah. Yes." I cracked my knuckles.

Brennan laughed. "You're a horrible liar, you know that?"

"I used to be great at it."

He shrugged. "Not exactly a skill worth having."

I nodded and craned my neck, looking for the ferry.

"We'll get there, Jalen," Brennan said.

I couldn't sit still. *Lost or left?* Stupid feet. "I know."

One of the Ellies jumped up and stood in front of us. "What if we *don't* get there—huh? Jalen, do you know what will happen if you fail one of these challenges? Did you even bother asking?" She crossed her arms over her chest and glared at me.

"No, I guess I didn't," I murmured. That outcome hadn't really occurred to me, not until that lottery ticket. I had no idea what would happen to me if I failed. I only knew that I didn't want to know. "But I can't exactly quit now."

The other Ellie scoffed. "Jalen won't fail. She knows what she's doing, don't you, Jalen?"

I didn't answer. I couldn't lie.

The first Ellie's face crumpled. I stood and hugged her, unsure if I was comforting a friend or walking into some sort of trap. "Please don't fail, Jalen," she whispered into my hair. "I don't want to find out what happens if you do."

It sounded almost—*almost*—like my best friend used to sound. What I wouldn't give to see her right now.

I bounced on the balls of my feet. *Lost or left?* "I won't."

Dillon clapped his hands together loudly and hopped off the bench next to us. "You guys are a bunch of *downers*. C'mon! Let's rock this joint!" He snatched up his tuba case and flipped open the shiny brass locks.

I winced—more locks. But Dillon pulled out a gleaming brass tuba—a smallish one, its horn the size of a basketball—and threw it over his head. He shimmied into it, then jerked his head at the trio of musicians that played next to the Louis Armstrong statue outside the terminal.

"Let's go!" He grinned his Cheshire cat grin. His ankle seemed to be feeling better. Which instantly made *me* feel better.

The trio—a trumpet player, a saxophonist, and a trombone player—had the trombone case sprawled open in front of them, catching spare change from the commuters headed to work on the ferry. The music their instruments made blended together like the ingredients for ice cream—sweet stuff that when combined made something cool and creamy and extra special. They smoothed right through Louis Armstrong's "What a Wonderful World."

The song wound down, and Dillon showed the trio his tuba. "Mind if we make it a quartet, fellas?" The musicians didn't say anything, but transitioned the music to "When the Saints Go Marching In." It was a big song that needed a big sound, like a tuba. Dillon hopped right in.

And he was *horrible*. His blasts and blurps bounced off the statue, off the metal side of the ferry terminal, and crashed into each other in midair. It was a catfight of musical notes—howling, yowling notes, notes so loud and so awful, it seemed impossible one human and one tuba could make them.

But he was having so much *fun*. He kicked his legs out in front of him, he twirled in circles, he swayed that honking tuba side to side. He hopped around on the sidewalk, his tuba burping forth brassy blasts. I couldn't help but get swept up in his joy. I started clapping along. Both Ellies danced.

Dillon took his mouth off his mouthpiece long enough to shout to Brennan, "Pick it up on the bucket, dude!" He pointed his tuba at a yellow bucket near the trombone player's feet.

Brennan blushed. I nudged him with my elbow. "Go on," I whispered in his ear. I felt him shiver. "You can't be any worse than Dillon."

Brennan grinned, nodded, and pointed at the bucket.

The trombone player smiled and nudged the bucket toward Brennan with his toe. He sat on the curb and tucked the yellow bucket upside-down between his knees.

Brennan's palms slid and whacked and thrummed a drumbeat so steady that I swear those musicians sat up taller, played faster. He knew exactly when to tilt the bucket to get a better boom from the thing. Between Brennan's drumming and Dillon's deafening tuba blurts, I couldn't stop grinning.

Bliss! Sunshine swelled through me, warming me to my fingertips and toenails. My cheeks began to ache from all the smiling, my stomach clenched from all the laughing.

Wasn't I headed somewhere? It could wait. This was too much fun. When was the last time I had *fun*? I deserved this.

And then, silence. The song came to an all-too-abrupt end, like screeching brakes on a car. The trio nodded. Dillon and Brennan had drawn a small crowd, a crowd that was forking over dollar bills.

Brennan stood, blushed. "Thanks, fellas."

The trombone player nodded. "Anytime, kid. You got a real heartbeat on those things, you hear?"

Brennan beamed. And I laughed. They didn't say a thing about Dillon's talent.

✳ ✳ ✳

"Ferry's here," Brennan said. "C'mon."

The boat chugged up and slipped into the dock. We

dragged ourselves toward the entrance. I wasn't sure if my hesitation came from fear of the Keepers or fear of the ferry.

The five of us—me, Brennan, Dillon, and the Ellies—crossed through the echoing metal terminal to get to the second story of the ferry. Below us, cars clanged and clattered onto the wide parking deck that took up the whole lower level. I jumped at every boom those cars made as they loaded onto the boat.

But I was doing it. I was getting onto the ferry! I hadn't made it this close to a boat in four years. I wished I could share this triumph with Ellie. But not only did I not know which Ellie was mine, she wouldn't remember my paralyzing fear of boats, anyway.

I used to love riding the ferry into the city. My dad once said it looked like a floating tiered wedding cake. A ferry ride always meant something exciting was in my future.

I felt someone staring at me. A petite woman with tight curls springing out from under a captain's hat. Rather, it was a horrible mesh baseball hat that read CAPTAIN in script. She wore an orange vest with yellow reflective strips on it, and she was studying me. I held my breath. No mist.

When we reached the ferry itself, I paused. I fought the urge to do what my dad used to do: He'd pause here, too, and yell, "Permission to board, Captain?" Every time. It made me howl with laughter when I was a kid. The other passengers would smile and laugh, too.

I looked around for some sign, something that would tell me to *stay off this boat*. Every time I'd tried to get on a boat since my dad had disappeared, I would see a sign, something warning me to stay away. Today—nothing. Were the signs still there and, as an Ophiuchus, I just couldn't see them now? Before, I would've seen a sign. Or maybe . . . would've made one up? But today, not even the huge orange patches of rust coating the vessel could turn me away.

I pushed back my shoulders and stepped over the inch-wide crack that separated the terminal from the boat, the crack that separated land from water. It felt like I was stepping over a canyon. I threw my head back and laughed.

The woman watching me, the captain, nodded and climbed the stairs to the steering room at the tip-top of the boat. Brennan, Dillon, the Ellies, and I entered the huge, hollow seating area. There weren't many people on board. I supposed this early on a Saturday morning was always slow.

Brennan and I plopped into chairs that looked like scoops of sherbet. Dillon dropped his tuba with a thud and fell into a nearby seat. He gripped his head and immediately turned a lovely shade of puke green. I thought of his ankle and sat up. "Are you okay?" I asked him. "You don't look so hot."

He swallowed, nodded, then swallowed again. "Boats. Water. Not my thing. Ferry ride's quick, though. I'll be alright." Brennan nodded with sympathy. And, boy, did I ever understand being afraid of boats.

The Ellies buzzed around Dillon like gadflies, asking,

"Are you alright, Dillon?" and "Do you need anything, Dillon?" One Ellie trying to out-Ellie the other. Maddening.

Seeing two Ellies here surprised me; I had hoped Fake Ellie would disappear around all these other humans. But even though it was a small crowd, it was still a crowd, where everyone makes a habit of overlooking everyone else. She didn't need to disappear in a crowd. It was probably very safe for her here.

My eyes closed almost immediately. The air smelled like fish and salt and mud—the earth-meets-river-meets-sea smell that always hung over New Orleans's riverfront. The gentle rocking took me back to my dad's boat, a small, rusted fishing thing that was barely big enough to be called a dingy. I inhaled. I'd missed this.

My chin knocked against my chest and my head snapped up. I needed to move, or risk falling asleep. Asleep! I couldn't make myself that vulnerable!

"Want to go for a walk?" I asked Brennan.

He nodded. We climbed the stairs to the third level of the ferry, the open-air level. Fresh air was what I needed.

At the top of the steel staircase, the woman from the terminal, the one wearing the captain's hat, looked down on us, hands on hips. We hadn't yet left the dock.

"You two come with me," she ordered. She turned and strode toward the next level of stairs, expecting us to follow. Brennan and I froze.

The captain paused, turned, and shifted what I thought

was a huge glob of chewing tobacco from one cheek to another. But then she blew a bubble, a huge, pink, quivering bubble. It popped with a snap when she sucked it back into her mouth.

"Come," she said around the wad in her mouth. She jerked her head toward the next set of stairs, to the very top of the ferry. "You'll want to see the steering room."

It wasn't a question. But she *was* being nice. She'd seen me hesitate before getting on the boat, and she wanted to help. And if I were being honest, *yes*, I wanted to see the steering room! I'd wanted to since I was a kid, since I first started thinking of this ferry as a big floating cake. Since my dad squatted down and pointed up, up, up at the flapping flags and the spinning radar thingies and said in a hush, "Jalen, *that's* where the captain stands." I nodded and followed.

The captain unlocked a chain strung across the next set of stairs. On the chain, a sign dangled: WARNING! RESTRICTED AREA! We climbed the stairs toward the captain's roost.

As I was climbing, I became woozy. My head felt like it was filled with whooshing air. I became very aware of how high above the water we were, how high in the air I now stood. Four stories up! I swallowed.

I'd never been afraid of heights before. In school I'd scale the rock wall to the roof of the gym. When we'd toured the local theater, I was the only one who'd been brave enough to climb out on the catwalk and learn about stage lighting. I froze and started shaking. The captain smiled and extended her hand down to me. I nodded, took it, and edged up the stairs. Her hand was callused from hard work.

✳ ✳ ✳

The captain stood behind the wheel, and the boat slowly chugged out of port. It was noisy, rattling progress—this old boat straining against the powerful Mississippi River current. But I was more comfortable inside this tiny room, surrounded by walls and gadgets.

And then I smiled to myself—I was *on a boat*. Once I looked past all the dials and gadgets and flashing lights, I noticed the view. It made me slightly dizzy at first, looking out. But this view of New Orleans couldn't be beat. The Crescent City Connection Bridge draped over the river to our left. I secretly stuck out my tongue at it—*See me, on a boat? I don't need you anymore, bridge!* The white spires of the Saint Louis Cathedral poked the sky, up and to the right. Straight ahead were the towering hotels and glittering buildings of downtown New Orleans, and the mirrory green roundness of the Audubon Aquarium.

"Take the wheel," the captain said. Her breath smelled pink. A long lock of her curly blond hair had freed itself from under the hat and hung past her shoulders.

My heart skipped. "Really?"

She smiled, a goofy, lopsided grin around her glob of gum. "Yes, *really*."

I stepped up to the wheel, a U-shaped thing, and paused

just before gripping it. I could feel the power leaping out of that captain's wheel into my fingers. The power to chart my own course. I'd be the one in control. It'd been so long since I felt in control. I *needed* this. *Deserved* it. My hands wrapped around the wheel. Orange warmth flamed inside me and energized me to my toes. I was steering the Algiers Ferry!

I turned, briefly, to look back at Algiers Point, slowly getting smaller behind us. It was so different from the downtown side of the river. Trees and grass and homes dotted the west bank. The expanse of water between us and land, between us and home, grew.

We were so vulnerable here.

"Look at that." The captain's voice beside me had turned from powdery pink to mirrored steel. "You've got water in your veins. Just like your dad."

My knuckles turned white on the steering wheel. *My dad?*

I realized now who I was up against. I should never have agreed to steer.

The captain fizzled away, disappearing into a thick fog that filled the room with sulfur stink. Brennan scrambled to unlock the door. The mist twirled and twined, the script on the baseball hat thinning out, then spiraling, solidifying into massive curled horns. The hair—long, flowing, golden curls that had been tucked under the hat—fell, then turned to near stone. A thick skull soon covered itself with smelly matted fur. Snorting nostrils, no longer breathing pink puffs of bubble-gum air but musty, gamy steam. Shoulders that stretched ever higher, over six feet. Hooves pounding on the metal floor of the steering room. A short, twitching tail.

The captain of this ship? Aries the ram.

* * *

Brennan had managed to make it out of the captain's room onto the stairs leading down to the seating area. But I had been greedy. I'd wanted to stand at the control panel—just this once—and feel like *I* was the one charting the course.

My instinct was to grab the stool behind me. It was, of course, bolted to the floor. The mist was clearing now, and the ram filled almost every inch of this room. Her flanks twitched. Rather, *his*. The female captain? Now a male ram. His head thrashed from side to side. I guessed the captain hadn't thought of the consequences of morphing into a ram in this tiny room. Impulsive. Just like an Aries.

In trying to turn, the ram's horn jammed in the ferry's control panel. Sparks shot forth. The lights flickered, and the hum of the engine died. There were just a handful of passengers below, but I heard their groans over the ram's snorts as the ferry lost power.

The ferry was drifting now. At the whim of the powerful Mississippi River. The Coast Guard would come soon. Was that good or bad?

Bad, I decided. They'd catch me and lock me in a room filled with questions. No time for that.

Brennan stood at the top of the narrow stairway leading down. "Jalen!" His voice sounded small, coming to me around this beast. There was nothing in this cabin to use as a weapon; everything was bolted down or attached. I'd have to squeeze past Aries to the door. And I had to do it now, while his horn was still trapped. I pressed against the wall and inched toward the exit.

Aries stomped his hooves, trying to free his jammed horn. The din of his feet pounding against the metal floor and echoing around this tiny room was deafening. The floor dented and warped. I hugged the wall and continued around the room, trying not to slide under those massive, crushing hooves.

The door was a few feet away now, but Aries's hindquarters blocked my exit. I put my hands on his wiry fur and pushed gently.

One does not push an Aries gently. His fury exploded, his hind legs bucking and kicking. The control panel sparked and fizzled. His mighty horns lifted toward the ceiling. He shook them with obvious pride. He had freed himself. I had to leave *now*.

He was trying to turn to face me. I pushed once more—no, *shoved*—his hindquarters and reached the doorway.

As I did, I was launched forward, chest first, like I had a

rocket pack strapped to my back. Pain exploded through me, back to front. Aries had kicked me, *hard*, onto the stairs. I instantly got dizzy, flying forward, four stories up. The sensation of being kicked coupled with being so high up made me feel as though I were sailing through the air for hours, rather than seconds. I gripped the first thing I saw.

Brennan. I landed on top of him, knocking his feet out from under him. Together we skidded, *thump, thump, thump* down the metal stairs.

At the bottom, I leaped to my feet, then pulled Brennan up. "You alright?"

He blinked, rubbed the back of his head, shook it off. "Yeah. I think."

I cocked my ear up at the stairwell; yes, the ram was still trapped in that small room for the moment. Our feet pounded down the next set of metal stairs and into the seating area.

"Ellie, Dillon—*Aries*."

Dillon's head popped up. "Where?"

But I didn't need to answer him. The banging on metal grew closer. Aries had freed himself from the room and was clomping down the stairs. He curled through the entryway and emerged from the stairwell, a majestic, horrible sight. He stood at the base of the stairs, scanned the lobby, and found us. His eyes tightened.

I slid my hand toward the nearest Ellie. "Give me the book," I whispered. Ellie slowly, painstakingly withdrew *The*

Keypers of the Zodiack and eased it toward me. Aries took in our every movement. But he wasn't readying himself to charge, not yet. He was enjoying watching us squirm.

I slowly flipped through the pages and found the entry:

> *"Aries, the ram. April 19—May 13. Thou art the leader of the Zodiack, Aries, and as such, thou hast the confidence, ambition, and determination to tackle the rocky challenges thou adorest. Thy will to succeed is so strong that thou canst be brash, impatient, and stubborn in thy pursuits. Yet thou art a master of finding solutions. Find one for thine own self! Thy legions of friends art more than eager to help, and thy confidence and enthusiasm ensure a lifetime of camaraderie. Make certain, however, that thine ambitions eclipse not thy friendships: Thou hast lost companions in thy quest to remain on top. Thou prize winning above all else, and thou will stop at naught to remain commander o'er all."*

I folded the book shut. I raised my eyes, locking into a staring contest with Aries. I didn't tear my eyes away to look about the ferry; I knew a handful of commuters were scattered around. Was this really where this Challenge would take place?

A brassy flash flared to my left. I thought I saw Dillon flip open his tuba case and yank the instrument out, but I didn't dare break my power stare with Aries to check. Really? His *tuba? Now?!*

The Ellie standing next to me seemed to be watching Dillon, too. "Go, Leo!" she shouted. "You can do this!"

I straightened and Aries snorted. I whipped toward Ellie. The look on her face told me she knew she'd made a huge mistake by saying that.

"Leo?" I asked. My gaze narrowed at her, at this fake. "What do you mean, *Leo?*"

But *I'd* made a mistake, too. I'd taken my eyes off Aries. I heard the pounding of hooves on metal, felt the floor vibrate from a mighty animal charging. Ellie shoved me, hard. "Move!" she yelled, and vanished. I landed on my tailbone and skidded across the metal floor of the ferry.

Massive, shell-like horns rammed into the metal side of the boat, punching a dent in the spot where I'd stood just seconds before. The ferry teetered in the water under the impact. A few passengers screamed. My heart thudded in my ears. I cut my eyes away from the thick yellow hooves of the beast just feet away and toward Dillon. He marched toward us, wearing his tuba, still greenish and swaying from the rocking boat. But he was doing a noble job fighting his seasickness.

"You've ruled the zodiac for long enough, Aries," he purred. "Time for new management."

And then he pounced. The brassy tuba flashed under the too-white neon lights of the ferry—*blam!*—like a firework, an explosion of light and mist. As Dillon flew through the air, he morphed. Through the fog I could see the shadow of his tuba, still around his waist, turn from shiny, solid brass into sleek, coarse fur and taut muscle. The circle of the tuba horn quivered and tossed, transforming into a magnificent mane. One last blast wailed through Dillon's horn, but it sounded less like a tuba and more like a . . . *roar*.

When he landed on soft, nimble paws, his metamorphosis was complete. He snarled.

Dillon was Leo, the lion. And he was here to take control of the zodiac.

Leo and Aries crouched and circled one another like two beasts in the wild, readying themselves to fight to the death. Except this was the wild of New Orleans. And these beasts couldn't exactly fight to the *death*, could they?

Ellie and Brennan eased over to me. Ellie—my wonderful, true friend Ellie. The fake Ellie had exposed herself, had vanished, but my *friend* was here. I squeezed her hand so tight I thought I might crush it. She tugged me toward the staircase. "Let them duke it out themselves," she whispered.

I nodded, but I knew immediately that it felt wrong. Aries snorted and shoved a twisted horn in Leo's face, showing off its size. He was bragging (like an Aries) that Leo's flesh was about to be ripped off its bones. Leo, in turn, growled a low, fierce grumble that filled the ferry like thunder. He was (like a Leo) telling Aries to bring it.

I couldn't let them fight. Somehow I knew—*I* had to be

the one to defeat them, or *I* would lose. And I couldn't just let Dillon—no, Leo!—take over the zodiac. There had been too many changes already. No, I'd have to intervene.

Leo, brash and bold, took the first swipe. With a roar, his sharp claws raked across Aries's flanks and left four raw, meaty rips across the flesh. Aries bellowed, writhed, and kicked Leo in the ribs. The crack of bone was sickening. Leo skidded across the metal floor with a whimper. The ferry rocked violently with the shift of bulk.

One of the other passengers screamed and pointed at us. "It's them! It's those three!" The other passengers nodded, their faces twisting in a flash, morphing from generic faces in a crowd to the soured faces of a mob.

I didn't have much time. I zipped through the copy of *The Keypers of the Zodiack* still in my sweaty hands.

"Leo, the lion. July 23–August 22. Leo, thou art a powerful force, though thy temperament shifts as the winds from creative to destructive. Thy demands to be at the center of all are usually rewarded, which makes thee confident and dignified, yet boastful and attention-seeking. The generosity thou possessest is not without fault, as thou demandest both recognition and appreciation. Thine instincts are akin to an animal's, not surprising, as pride defines thee above all. Thy dependence on risk and luck, while exciting and entertaining to all, can make thy friends feel like mere props in thy games. Be warned that thou

art prone to overlook small details, and that oft results in loss. Beware all distractions, Leo. Like the cat for which thou art named, thy distractions are many and potentially deadly."

Aries had speared Leo with the tip of his horn and hefted him to his feet, goading him to keep fighting. Leo was weak, I realized, from being on this ferry. Cats and water—not a good mix. This battle would end quickly if I didn't do something fast.

The two beasts tossed and tumbled and growled while the ferry rocked and swayed and pitched; no way could I step in the middle of all those teeth and horns and claws. I looked around the ferry for something, *anything* I could use as a weapon. I found nothing.

And then I saw it, the thing that had been my most powerful weapon all night. In my very own hands.

I held the copy of *The Keypers of the Zodiack* over the side of the boat. Of the two, I knew which would be more likely to take this bait. I whistled a shrill, loud blast. Whistled! Another thing I'd never been able to do before.

Both beasts froze and turned their black eyes to me. Both saw the book—*their* book, *The Keypers of the Zodiack*— at risk. I wriggled the book with my wrist, teasing the two animals. Sure enough, Leo's eyes tore away from Aries and followed every twitch of the text.

"Here, kitty kitty," I whispered. Leo crouched, ready to pounce on the book.

He snarled and his fangs glinted. His tail cracked like a whip. Then his black eyes narrowed and shifted to me. He roared, announcing that he was about to pounce on his prey.

Me. His prey was me.

No, no, no! This was not the plan! "Leo!" I said, waving the book madly. His eyes were drawn back to it. "Here, kitty!"

Hope I'm right about this, I thought.

"Come and *get it!*" I hurled the book overboard. The pages flapped in the wind, down, down, down toward the mighty, muddy Mississippi.

And Leo leaped.

"Dillon!" Ellie screamed.

"The book!" Brennan yelled.

Leo scrambled over the guardrail and jumped after the book. He curled back his lips, bared his mighty teeth, and sank them into the pages of the book. He splashed into the river with the impact of a car crash.

Aries bellowed behind us and charged. The three of us scattered like drops of blood as Aries drove his horn into the guardrail. The four-inch metal crushed under the weight of his blow. He struggled to right himself after his battle with Leo.

I had just enough time to look down to where Leo had landed in the river. His paws clawed at the surface, grasping for something solid. His lion's body looked small, sharp, pointed when wet, rather than the sleek, muscular shape he had when dry. He tried to roar one final time but ended up sinking below the murky water. His roar reached us in a sickening gurgle. My heart squeezed. I hoped Dillon didn't feel a thing.

A tear slid down Ellie's cheek. "Bye, Dillon."

The water began to burble and boil, and off the surface rose a fog-like mist. A burst of light shone below the murky depths. Leo shot forth in a gush and pranced toward the heavens. But unlike the others, he paused. He looked back at us, and Dillon's voice came through in a roar: "Thanks for being such fun playthings."

✳ ✳ ✳

Leo's birthstone clanked to the floor of the ferry. Aries pounced and kicked it. It slid like a hockey puck toward the edge of the boat and clinked against the guardrail, threatening to topple into the river. Brennan dove for it and scooped it up just before it plummeted into the water. He tossed the stone to me. The birthstone was smooth, fiery orange. It took my breath away, that orange stone. It was just like my new world.

"*Sic itur ad astra,*" I chanted. Dillon's stone disappeared, bubbling on the palms of my hands.

My chant was stolen by the clamoring of hooves across the metal seating area. Aries was charging, head lowered, right horn leading the charge, right shoulder cocked forward to deliver the mighty blow.

We dove aside. Aries tangled himself in a twist of plastic seats.

Ellie grabbed my hand. "On the next charge, go downstairs," she whispered. Brennan nodded.

Aries freed himself, and his black eyes locked on me. I saw in those black eyes that he not only hated me because I was the Challenger, he hated me for bringing Leo straight to him. Aries scratched the metal floor with his right front hoof, and it sounded like fingernails on a chalkboard. My teeth ached at the sound.

In one swift move, Aries lifted his two front legs off the ground, cocked his head and his shoulder, and propelled himself at us like a battering ram. The three of us dashed toward the stairs that led to the lowest level of the ferry. Just before we reached the stairs, the ferry listed again under the impact of Aries's blow. Brennan lost his footing and slipped backward. Ellie grabbed his shirt collar and dragged him into the stairwell.

We dashed to the lower level, slamming against the handrails of the stairs as the boat bobbed in the river. Car horns were blaring now, alarms blasting under the jarring force of Aries's mighty horns. Drivers stood next to their cars, shouting, "What's going on up there?"

A voice crackled through the emergency intercom

system: "All passengers report to the middle deck. Repeat, all passengers to the second level, immediately." The voice sounded suspiciously like Gemini's. The drivers of the cars filed upstairs. We would soon be alone with Aries.

The thundering sound of hooves on metal pounded above us. I hoped all those passengers up there were safe. But I knew Aries would follow us. He wasn't interested in them. It was *me* he was after.

Ellie led us to a metal lifeboat strapped with ropes to some kind of crane-and-pulley system. She began fumbling with the knots to untie them.

"We need a knife," I said. I scanned the parking deck of this ferry. Half a dozen cars, but no knife.

Aries had learned from his mistakes. He had morphed back into the captain for this set of stairs. She emerged from the staircase disheveled and panting, jaw jutting forward.

"What do you know?" the captain huffed. "You *fight* like your father, too." In a flash, human morphed into ram. My teeth clenched.

Aries, the ram, bounded onto the nearest car, crushing it. He leaped from that car to the next one, the one parked nearest us, in an obvious display of might. Glass flew everywhere, glittering, twinkling, dangerous.

"Ja-*len*," Ellie warned. She'd only freed two of the knots with her shaking hands. "I need more time!"

A large shard of mirror flew end over end and skidded

under a car parked two spaces up. I shielded my head. "Be right back."

"Jalen!" Brennan yelled. But I'd already scurried up one car, crouching next to the passenger side. Aries caught sight of me and sprang, crunching the car I was huddled against. The tires exploded. Gasoline soaked me, its smell choking, its fumes blinding. Gas poured into my cuts, stinging like fire.

I could see the gleaming shard of mirror under the car ahead. I had to get to it. I tried to stand but slipped in the gasoline spill. Aries was taking aim, preparing to pounce down on me. I finally managed to get a toehold and push myself forward through the slick gas. I slid under the car ahead of me. I grabbed the shard of glass, cutting my hand I gripped it so tight.

I had surprised Aries, but not for long. He adjusted his leap, and I saw his underbelly fly overhead as I skidded out from under the car, just seconds before it crumpled.

I tossed the shard to Brennan. "Cut the rope!"

He caught the shard of mirror, thankfully. If he hadn't caught it, it would have shattered and been useless.

By the time I scrambled back to Ellie and Brennan, they'd cut the ropes and were maneuvering the lifeboat into the river. It landed, one story down, in the water. We had to jump *now*, before the lifeboat floated too far away in the rapid current.

Ellie grabbed an orange life jacket from a metal locker, scrambled over the guardrails, and jumped first.

Brennan climbed to the top of the guardrail but froze, clutching his life vest. He was visibly shaking and it occurred to me that *this* Brennan was terrified of water.

I was suddenly struck with flashes of a memory. Brennan was ten; I was eight. A group of kids at Lake Pontchartrain, at a rope swing. Let go of the rope, land in the lake. I was too chicken to try. Brennan insisted that the other kids stop clucking at me. He winked and whispered, "You don't have to try it, but you should." I remember him slipping into the lake with barely a splash. And I remember that after that, I tried it.

"Sorry, Brennan, but you'll thank me later," I said. I pushed him over the edge.

At the top of the guardrail, I looked back at Aries. He had freed himself from the gnarled metal of the car and was taking aim.

I didn't have the same luxury, the one of taking aim. I grabbed a life jacket off the wall and jumped, shoving my fear of how high up I was aside.

I screamed the whole way down. It was a bad idea, because when I smacked against the water, I immediately realized I wanted that air back. I kept sinking, deeper and deeper into the cold dirty water. There was no bottom to hit and push off of; it was miles below. I opened my eyes for an excruciating moment. Brown water flooded my vision.

Then the forces of nature shifted with a jerk thanks to the life jacket I clutched. My neck snapped back with the change. I stopped sinking, paused, then rocketed up. I kicked toward the direction I hoped would let me find air. My lungs were on fire with strain.

When I finally broke through the surface, I gulped in buckets of air. Ellie and Brennan were a few feet away from me, inside the boat. Both dry—they'd both made good jumps. They hauled me over the side.

I'd been underwater long enough to give Aries an advantage. He had stripped away the guardrails with his massive curled horns, and now he stood above us, just a few feet away. One leap into this tiny metal boat and we'd all drown.

Aries's mouth curled into a snarl. He had us trapped and he knew it. He shook his heavy shell-shaped horns with pride, reared onto his hind legs, and *pushed*.

There was nothing else to do. I was *not* going to let my friends get hurt.

I'd come this far. I supposed I should be proud of that. I only wished I didn't have to let down my mom, my Nina.

From my crouch, I shouted, "I surrender! You win!"

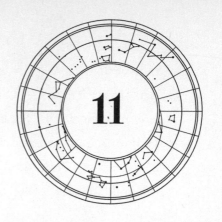

11

I heard Ellie's sharp intake of breath beside me.

What would become of me now? Where would the Keepers take me? What happens after the After? Would it be peaceful, heavenly where I was headed? Or would it be a deep, dark, sinister place, black as night? Black as Keeper eyes?

But instead of the crushing weight of Aries, instead of a watery grave sucking us to the bottom of the river, instead of being buried alive under the thousands of pounds of silt gushing through the Mississippi River, a loud thunk sounded. I opened one eye, then another.

A diamond. Aries's birthstone.

The ram trotted into the heavens, shaking those mighty horns with pride. His winning streak was intact.

I had let Aries win. That's all she/he wanted. To win. Over and over again. In letting Aries win, I had won.

With shaky hands, I lifted the clear, gleaming diamond

into the early morning sky, still hazy pink around the edges of day. *"Sic itur ad astra."*

Brennan chuckled. "Smart move, Jalen."

Half my mouth grinned, but it was forced. I hadn't meant to win. I had truly wanted to surrender. Did Aries know that? Would it have worked otherwise? My stomach flopped. *I had quit.*

This new doubt doused some of my fire, leaving behind an unwelcome pile of ash. Would I have the strength to fight the eight remaining Keepers?

"But the book—" Brennan started. Ellie grinned and reached into her messenger bag. She pulled out her copy of *The Keypers of the Zodiack.*

"Two copies, ever since the other Ellie came around," I managed to explain. "I was hoping that was a detail Dillon would overlook. I mean Leo." We were silent at the mention of Dillon's name.

"The copy I threw overboard was from Fake Ellie," I said to change the subject. "Disposable. We'll still have two copies once she reappears, I imagine."

The other Ellie. She'd been in on Dillon's secret the whole time, I realized. She'd led us back to him, hurt at the bulldozer. And Dillon! He'd recovered so easily after he'd been hurt. He'd stopped the busses from running, he'd led us to believe he was *real.* He'd tricked us, used us to get to Aries. We *had* been his playthings.

Brennan sighed. "Let's go." He revved the boat's tiny outboard motor. "The boat's leaking."

In my daze, I looked down at the silver bottom of the boat. Sure enough, the muddy river was pushing into a tear in the seam. One of the rivets must have come loose with the impact of the birthstone. Over my shoulder, I saw the flashing lights of the Coast Guard as their boat sped toward the Algiers Ferry.

✳ ✳ ✳

We puttered toward land. We headed back to the West Bank, where we'd started. It was much closer, and it would have been near impossible to fight this river's mighty current to reach the opposite shore in this tiny boat. We dragged ourselves on shore and lay on the riverbank. I was shivering so bad my muscles spasmed, though I wasn't sure if it was from the cold river or my surrender or my confusion over who was what.

"I want to call my mom," I said. If I could find some small inkling of drill sergeant left in her, I'd be renewed. We'd come ashore near the ferry station and inside were clusters of pay phones. Ellie, luckily, had a quarter in her messenger bag.

This time, my mom answered on the first half ring.

"Jeremy? Is that you? I've been trying to reach you. I just don't think—I can't keep going without you."

Hearing my mom say my dad's name, hearing her admit such desperation, made my heart fall. I swallowed and replaced the phone back on the hook. I found a sunny spot in the grass and lay down. My surrender played over and over through my brain.

* * *

A crowd of people was setting up for a party in the park. A wedding—a sunrise wedding overlooking the river.

A head appeared above me. I couldn't see the face; the bright morning sun behind the person masked his face in shadows. I bolted upright, fists clenched, jaw tight to keep from chattering.

It was—who? How did I know this person? Oh, I used to be so good at recalling names and knowing faces before.

"The man from the bus stop," one of the Ellies whispered. Two Ellies again. I'd let another opportunity to note Real Ellie slip by. Another shiver raced through me.

The man shoved his face close to mine and pulled back his chapped lips, showing his gray teeth. Was he smiling or sneering?

"Is Henry there bothering you, kid?" another man called from across the lawn. I looked from the grungy, stinking man hovering over me to a group of what appeared to be his co-workers. The crowd of people, all wearing the same uniform this guy was wearing, paused to stare at us. I unclenched my fists, my teeth. They could *see* him. The whole crowd. He was real.

I shook my head and stood, dusting myself off. "No," I said, peering around this dirty man, this man who stood too close. "We're all right." The crew nodded and continued unloading white folding chairs.

The man from the bus stop thrust four huge tablecloths at me and motioned for us to wrap ourselves in them. His uniform was a golf shirt with a catering-company logo on it—NOLA NOM NOMS.

"He is and she is and he is and she is," he spit at me. He jerked his greasy hair at Gemini, who was now standing nearby. "He is and she is and—"

"You can see," I whispered. My pulse raced. How could he see the Keeper?

He nodded. "He is." I felt my eyes grow wide as he said it again. "He is."

I realized who he meant. "Dillon," I said. "You were right when you told us before, at the bus stop. He is. A Keeper." I sighed and pointed with my thumb at Gemini. "And so is she."

He turned to the pair of Ellies and started trembling. "No, no, no. Two there. Not one. Two there. Not one."

I sighed. "I know. Two Ellies. Can you—?"

He shook his head violently, as if he knew I was going to ask him which Ellie was real and which was pretend. He didn't want to make a guess, either.

I finally stopped shivering, huddled under that warm tablecloth. The man motioned for us to follow him, and we did. He scuttled around the catering truck. He grabbed a bunch of bananas, four beignets, and four steaming cups of coffee.

"Dude, thanks," Brennan said. We ate like we'd never seen food before. The beignets were still warm. The dough and powdered sugar melted on my tongue.

"Sir?" I asked after we'd eaten. He whipped around at the sound of my voice like I'd slapped him upside the head. I jerked back my arm like I might punch him. Instinct. But slowly, he raised his hands, palms open.

"Do you have any more of those shirts and pants?" I pointed to his NOLA NOM NOMS shirt. My clothes were wet, and Brennan and the Ellies still reeked of crab guts.

He held up a finger—*one moment*—and left, hugging himself and muttering. "Two there. Not one. Two." He returned a few minutes later with long-sleeved shirts and khaki cargo pants for us. Mine were way too long and had to be cuffed four times. Brennan's were way too short, and he and I chuckled that he looked like Michael Jackson. I unfastened Nina's pin from the T-shirt I was wearing and clasped it over my heart, just above the NOLA NOM NOMS logo.

We were fed and dry, and we needed to move on. I decided to extend my hand in handshake. "Thank you, sir."

He ignored my hand but nodded at us, then at Gemini.

"Two there. Not one." Two." He turned and twitched away. The other caterers chuckled at him.

When had he become so broken? Had he been like that prior to the personality shift?

Or had I done that to him?

* * *

"So . . . now what?" Brennan asked. I was glad someone asked it. I wasn't sure what we should do next.

"Wait for the next ferry?" I knew as I was saying it that the idea would get nixed.

"No," an Ellie said. "No ferry." The other Ellie shook her head in agreement.

We stood near the back of the park, behind the rows of guests at the wedding. I thought we were being quiet until the bride turned toward us.

"Shhhhh!" she hissed. Her eyebrows furrowed in a deep V. "Can't you see I'm getting married here?" The bride turned back to her groom, her face transforming from a sneer to a smile. She looked up at her husband-to-be with a huge, moony grin.

My face grew hot. "Sorry!" I whispered. The bride whipped toward me again.

"Jalen!" she whispered through gritted teeth. "I'll be *with* you in a *moment!*" The bride motioned with her head at the preacher, the groom. The preacher, oblivious to the bride's interruptions, welcomed everyone to this momentous occasion with a booming "Dearly Beloved, we are gathered here today . . ." The groom never looked away from his bride, adoring her so fully, it was almost like watching someone bleed. Come to think of it, none of the guests turned to see who the bride addressed, either.

The bride was a Keeper.

One of the Ellies was a step ahead of me, already flipping through *The Keypers of the Zodiack*. "Virgo. My new sign," she said, skimming the page. "Here it is." She read.

> "*Virgo, the maiden. Virgo, thou art modest, conscientious, industrious—everything a pet of thine elders is expected to be. This can make thy peers see thee as distant and unworthy of their trust, questioning thy motives. But not to worry—thou shalt win o'er most with thy charm and ceaseless wit. Love, to thee, is something to withhold to only the truly deserving; deep and true relationships art rare for thee. Thou prizest honesty, and thy keen eye can see order in the midst of chaos. Take note that thine obsessions and ambitions can plant the seed of distrust deep in thy heart. Should that cynicism take root, thou canst be fully and wholly uncooperative.'*"

Ellie snapped the book shut. "Uncooperative?" Her bottom lip stuck out. I, coincidentally, bit mine.

"Keep it *down* back there!" Virgo slammed her bouquet against her thigh. Daisy petals rained onto the platform.

The preacher, oblivious to that outburst, continued, "If anyone here knows why these two should not be married today, speak now or forever hold your peace."

Gemini whipped out her nail file and began sawing it across her fingertips. "I do. That sneak *cannot* get married. She's *Virgo*, for heaven's sake. It's against the laws of nature."

At that, Virgo stomped off the platform and stormed down the aisle, striding toward us. All the guests remained facing forward, listening to the preacher prattle on. The groom turned to watch his beloved walk away, but he was so far gone, he just grinned goofily at her antics.

"Poor sucker," Brennan said under his breath, lifting his chin at him.

Virgo came back and pushed Gemini in the chest with her bouquet. "You just couldn't let me have my first kiss, could you? Could you?! Jalen wouldn't have known!"

Gemini's face tightened. "Do *not* push me. And do you really think tricking your Challenger is the best way to win, Virgo? You're smarter than that, are you not? I know Jalen is."

Virgo slammed her bouquet to the ground in a pile of petals. Her black glare shifted from Gemini to me, back to Gemini. "Are you telling me—you're *helping* her? This . . . this . . . *kid*?"

Gemini paused, and it was a near deadly hesitation. Virgo slid her breezy wedding dress up to reveal a frilly blue garter. There, tucked in the garter, was a knife with a pearlized handle. In one swift move, she whisked it from her makeshift holster, wrapped around Gemini, and raised the sleek blade to Gemini's throat.

But Gemini was swift as well. She flicked her metal nail file up toward her neck, blocking the knife blade from slicing into her skin. It was a weak shield against Virgo's sharp weapon.

"What's to stop me from eliminating you from the zodiac right now?" Virgo said. She jerked her headlock even tighter around Gemini. Cords in both their necks strained. "Huh? Tell me? Why not just get rid of you once and for all?"

The silvery sheen of the knife's blade flashed. Such power-hungry beings these Keepers were! I stepped forward.

"You can't do this," I said, my voice low but growling. "It's not fair."

Virgo smirked at me. "Fair? What a child you are! Fair!" Every heaving laugh of Virgo's made Gemini strain as she tried to hold back that knife's edge.

"Fair," I repeated with a nod. Oh, what had her horoscope said? "It's not *honest*."

"Honest!" Virgo tossed Gemini aside. Our guide crumpled to the ground. My pulse slowed its pounding a bit. "Honesty? Is that what you want this to be about, Jalen?" She scooped up her bouquet and backhanded my head with it. "Then honesty you'll get. *You* get to decide."

I took a wavering breath to douse my anger and plucked a

petal from my hair. "Decide what?" I asked. "And how come that guy can see you?" I pointed to the groom. The groom had been watching Virgo like she was a perfect present, a surprise with a bow on top.

Virgo snapped around to look at the man in the tuxedo waiting at the altar. Her face softened. "It's love, Jalen. Just like any kind of love. He sees what he wants to see of me."

I blinked. Was that true? Do we see only the parts of others we want to see, both good and bad? I motioned toward the guests. "And them? What do they see?"

"They see two people in love." Virgo's eyes narrowed and she smirked. "Don't you believe in true love, Jalen?"

So this was it. What I had to decide. My Challenge was to decide if Virgo's love was true, pure. Or if she—a *Keeper*, a thing so adaptable it could imitate my best friend and I couldn't tell the difference—if *she* was faking it.

Virgo leaned close. "Allow me that kiss, Jalen," she whispered. She smelled like sticky-sweet flower petals. "It *is* true love." She gathered my hand in hers.

"I can give you true love, too," she said. She glanced over my shoulder at Brennan, then winked at me. My face flamed.

"True love." Virgo looked down at my hand and linked my pinkie finger with hers. She lifted our knotted fingers, then pulled her knife out from behind her bouquet. The blade rested at the base of my knuckle. "For the price of a finger."

I saw the horror written on my face in the blade of that knife, and yanked my hand away. Virgo tossed her head back with laughter. She was just trying to scare me, confuse me. Right?

Gemini shook her head. "Jalen, you cannot allow Virgo that kiss. She must remain totally innocent."

Virgo huffed, reached in the folds of her wedding gown, and produced a large blue sapphire, her birthstone.

"Jalen," she whispered, pressing it into my hands. All her teasing had evaporated. "I was using this as my something blue, but I trust you with it. I trust that you'll allow me my first kiss."

She turned and climbed back onto the platform, scooped up the groom's hands, and pressed them against her heart. But she furrowed her eyes at the groom. "Straighten up, William. This *is* your wedding, you know." He straightened his back into a line.

Gemini shook her head, the nail file twiddling between her fingers. "No. No, Jalen, she's playing you for a fool. You must cast her to the skies. Now."

The preacher turned to the groom. "Do you, William, take Virginia to be your lawfully wedded wife?"

The groom, William, glowed. "I most certainly do."

Gemini was pacing now. "Jalen, cast her to the skies!"

Virgo looked at me with tear-brimmed eyes. "Please, Jalen? Just a few more minutes?" Was she truly in love? Or was she an excellent actress? Oh, who knew!

I looked to the closest Ellie, who motioned to Gemini. "I'd do what Gemini says, Jalen." I threw my head back. I knew better than to ask an Ellie. That would just confuse me more.

A tear slid down Virgo's cheek.

The preacher continued. "Do you, Virginia, take William to be your lawfully wedded husband?"

She nodded and could barely squeak out the words past her tears. "Of course I do. No one else would have me." The crowd of guests chuckled at her charm.

I turned to Brennan. "What do you think?"

Brennan's head swiveled from Gemini to Virgo as though he were watching a tennis match. "Gemini says it's the law, Jalen. I'm not so sure we want to go breaking any laws."

This, from the guy who had been driving since he was thirteen. Orange fire swelled inside me. Why couldn't I tell?

Virgo and William exchanged rings. William slid a big sapphire ring on Virgo's finger and said, "With this ring, I thee wed. I offer you my hand and my heart, as I know they will be safe with you. All that I am I give to you, and all that I have, I share with you."

My heart tightened. My mother and my father had once said these same vows to each other, long before me. I'd seen their cheesy wedding video, with its bad lighting and awful hairdos. Had they truly been in love? Yesterday, based on my mother's boiling resentment, I would've said no.

He left when I was sick, so sick I was in intensive care, tied to a bed with tubes and machines of my own. So sick the doctors had told Mom and Dad that they'd tried everything, that nothing else could be done, that they should expect the worst. *That's* when my dad left. Mom carried so much anger about it. I remember Mom's face changing when she told me Dad was gone. It never changed back.

But now—now, it seemed, she was leaving us all to find him. She had loved him. She still did. She just had a funny way of showing it before.

"Jalen—" Gemini said, alarm in her tone.

"Jalen, please!" Virgo begged.

I raised the birthstone over my head.

"You have declared your everlasting love with the exchange of rings," the preacher said. "I now pronounce you husband and wife."

Before, I would cast Virgo to the skies now. Before, I followed the rules.

"You may kiss the bride."

William reached up and cupped his bride's chin ever so gently with his fingertips. He *saw* her. Without the book, without the key. He *saw.*

How do you ever know if another person loves you? Truly? You just have to believe it when they say they do. It's all we've got. I had to believe she saw him, too. I had to believe that.

Gemini turned her head.

Lips touched, soft and perfect.

"*Sic itur ad astra,*" I whispered.

Virgo was swept to the heavens, her veil a trail of light. She left one very confused groom standing alone. My insides twisted, watching him watch her disappear.

"Thank you, Jalen," Virgo's voice whispered soft as a sigh. Behind us, metal cages clacked open, and hundreds of white doves spiraled into the sky behind her. They were breathtaking, swooping, swirling, wings pumping open, flapping closed. Open, closed. Tiny flying heartbeats, each one.

"Virginia?" William was now shouting. "Virginia!"

Looking up, I had missed spotting the cat lurking under the bushes nearby. But now, this creature, orange and speedy, pounced into the air, wriggling and writhing to get ever higher.

His sharp teeth locked around one of the doves and dragged it back down to earth, a spray of blood and a tangle of feathers leading the way. He groaned a mangy, stray-cat groan, but he was wearing a flashy collar and appeared to be well-fed, his fur sleek. There was no reason this cat needed that dove.

"Virginia?" the groom wailed, his cries echoing the cat's.

What had I done? His new bride, now gone, forever. Would it have been easier for him if I'd cast Virgo to the skies before the kiss? But I'd made the right choice, right? Virgo had disappeared. And yet . . .

I looked down at the weight in my hands. The cool blue

stone glistened in the morning sun. Virgo's birthstone remained with me.

In a panic, I showed Gemini the flashing blue sapphire.
"Did I lose? Why do I still have the stone?"

"I don't know." Gemini was stunned. "I've never seen
this happen before."

I couldn't take my eyes off the stone, heavy in my hands.

One of the Ellies whistled long and low.

"That is one massive gem," she whispered over my shoulder. "Imagine what you could buy with that."

My mind flew to the pile of medical bills teetering in our
kitchen corner, the bills from Nina and the leftover bills from
me, years old, screaming at us in red-red ink to be paid—
now. This stone *could* help with those and with our fine, old
home crumbling around them.

But, no, surely that's not why Virgo left her stone behind. I shook my head. That just didn't feel right.

The wedding party, the guests, milled around, wondering
at the bride's abrupt departure. Finally, I turned to Brennan
to ask him what he thought.

But he was gone. Both of the Ellies, too.

"Ellie?" I asked. I heard panic in my own voice. "Brennan? Where are you guys?"

The park was a knot of people searching for others. I
tucked the birthstone into the cargo pocket of my new kha-
kis and made my way back to the main road. Then I saw it.

A black car.

Orange flames surged in my stomach.

Gemini grabbed my elbow. "Don't trust them," she said before fading away. "Don't."

At that moment, a single arrow whizzed through the air and planted itself with a *sproing* in the dirt between my feet. Sagittarius was near. The tip of the arrow buried itself several inches deep, the shaft waggling from the impact. If an arrow like that could dig into hard earth so easily, I could only imagine what it could do to soft flesh.

The back door of the car swung open, and Agent Cygnus leaned across Ellie and Brennan.

"Jalen," he called. "I think you should get in."

12

We walked under a dotted line of fluorescent lights down a long hallway and through a heavy metal door. It banged shut with an echo.

"Have a seat," Agent Cygnus said. He swept his hand at a long table with dozens of cheap folding chairs scattered around it. The lights buzzed overhead. We sat.

The black car had taken us backward, backward, away from the river to a government-looking building with no windows. I guessed we were near the naval base. I guessed we just lost two miles in two minutes. The orange inside flickered.

"Can I get you anything? Something to eat, maybe?" Agent Cygnus said. Ellie shook her head sharply. One Ellie, thankfully, since we'd climbed into that dark car. I clutched her hand. This was *my* Ellie.

Agent Cygnus leaned his chair back and propped his wing-tip shoes on the table. I thought about how much

damage I could do with a pair of pointy-toed shoes like that.
I was totally losing it.

Agent Griffin joined us, spinning his chair around and
leaning over the back of it like a hungry wolf staring at
meat. I thought I saw a leather holster strapped to his side.
"How did you do it?" he grumbled, shaking his head at me.
"How did a kid like you unlock the Keepers? We've been
trying for years."

Agent Cygnus banged forward in his chair and shot Griffin a look that said all too plainly, *Shut up!* He turned to me
and his face softened. "Nothing at all? A soda?"

I didn't have time for this. "How did you find me?" I
asked. "Originally, I mean."

Agent Cygnus smiled again. "Yes. Let's see. We'll start
at the beginning, shall we?"

I couldn't tell if he was taunting me. "Just make it quick.
I'm on a deadline." Wowza! Me, talking to government of-
ficials like that. I hoped I wasn't about to be handcuffed.

His face grew serious. Maybe even miffed. "Of course.
Well, finding you was easy enough. We simply traced the
ultraviolet patterns that the Keepers leave behind in their
travels. They led directly to your doorstep. They faded after
scattering throughout the city."

They knew about the Keepers, even though they couldn't
see them. "You traced ultraviolet patterns," I repeated.

Agent Cygnus nodded. "It's part of what our agency does."

"Are you . . ." I felt silly even asking it. "FBI?"

Agent Cygnus chuckled, stood, and tugged his jacket lapel. "No. Not FBI. We spend a little more time . . . *stargazing*, if you will."

"Like NASA?" Brennan asked.

Agent Griffin snorted. "No. *Not* like NASA."

Agent Cygnus scowled at his partner, then turned back to me. "We're a little more discreet than that."

Discreet? Sounded very secretive to me. I hesitated before asking my next question, because honestly, I'm not sure I wanted to know. "What do you want?"

Agent Cygnus paced the cold tile floor. "You're aware that every personality on earth has shifted, aren't you, Jalen?" he asked.

I shrugged, unsure of what exactly I should admit to knowing.

"Jalen!" Agent Griffin slammed his fist on the metal table. His coffee sloshed out.

Agent Cygnus looked at him and shook his head, then continued, "This shift has major consequences. Surgeons are suddenly squeamish and refusing to perform surgery. Airline pilots are afraid to fly. And our world leaders are now timid, or aggressive, or lax. Over the past few hours, several enemy countries have escalated toward war." He leaned on his knuckles, glaring at me. "Jalen, world peace is at stake."

World peace. Those words sank in, turning my insides

from sharp orange to steely metallic. I tried to swallow but couldn't.

People across the globe, unfit for their jobs, unfit for their lives.

Somehow I forced my voice through the dust in my throat. "I understand. You need me to switch everyone back." I stood, reenergized by this new information.

Agent Cygnus eyed me, and it was like he could see Virgo's blue birthstone tucked into my pocket. Instinctively I touched the side of my pants leg.

"Oh, you don't understand the half of it, Jalen." His eyes were unblinking. "Take a seat."

I did, and Agent Cygnus continued. "What we *need*," he said, "is Ophiuchus's stone."

The stone? He didn't mention the pin I was wearing, the lock, the book. He wanted the stone? It occurred to me that these agents really *didn't* know how to unlock the Keepers, or the consequences of what happened when you did. They just knew about the stones, it seemed.

"Jalen, that stone?" Agent Cygnus was staring at me so hard, I felt like he was trying to hurt me with his eyes. "It can cure anything. Even death."

My eyes clamped shut, my chest clamped shut, my brain clamped shut. Ophiuchus held more than the power to shift our personalities. Ophiuchus held the secret to death.

"Immortality?" I hadn't realized I'd whispered it out loud until Agent Cygnus answered me.

"Not exactly," he said. "The stone doesn't prevent death or illness. But it can reverse it. The ultimate cure."

That was why the Keepers protected Ophiuchus so adamantly. *That* was why the sign was no longer a part of the zodiac, why it was hidden away in the history books. Why the Other Twelve descended to earth and committed to battle anyone who unlocked it, anyone who threatened the order of the universe. What human would need to rely on a horoscope sign, or really *any* higher power, if the ability to control death was in our hands? Ophiuchus could alter humanity, forever. It was the most powerful sign of them all.

What humans would do if they had power over death! For a flash, it sounded marvelous: *a world where death could be cured*. I instantly thought of my Nina. I suddenly wanted nothing else but *that stone in my hand*.

But . . . even if death could be reversed, ours wouldn't be a world without pain. If anyone knew that pain could exist without the immediate threat of death, it was me. In fact, a single stone that could cure the dead would probably *cause* more suffering than it could heal. Who *wouldn't* fight for that kind of power? The greed it would cause! The wars and destruction!

And surely not everyone would have eternal life. No, *that* kind of stone in *our* kind of world? The power over death would be reserved for the richest, the strongest. Or the evilest, the kind of person who would stop at nothing for the chance to pick and choose who lives and who dies.

No. The agents were right. Humans could not be trusted with that kind of power.

"But we don't know where Ophiuchus is," Brennan whispered at last.

I opened my eyes. Agent Cygnus was still glaring at me. "But you think you do, don't you? Otherwise you wouldn't be on this quest. Find her. Find her stone. The stone has all the power. Find Ophiuchus's stone and bring it to us. I don't care how long it takes. We must ensure that this never happens again. We have to destroy that stone. If that stone falls into the wrong hands . . ."

As Agent Cygnus talked, Agent Griffin pulled something out of a paper bag. A pot—one of *my pots*. He plunked it onto the table, not caring if he might shatter it.

Just the sight of the pot made me feel ill. It was hollow and empty that pot. I wasn't that person anymore, the person who so desperately needed to make them.

Agent Cygnus's mouth pulled into a straight line. He bent toward me and his jacket fell open, showing, yes, a holster. His breath was icy, like peppermint. "This isn't the first time this has happened." His fingers twitched. I flinched. "But you already knew that, didn't you, Jalen?"

My heart tightened. I felt myself nodding, agreeing. Aries had said, *"You fight like your father."* I had known then.

My dad disappeared when I was nine. I was on the edge of my own death, and my father disappeared, and my mother hardened bone-dry like this pot.

Had he unlocked Ophiuchus to try to heal me?

And if *he* hadn't survived these Challenges, how could *I*?

"You must do this, Jalen," Agent Cygnus was saying. "And we're here to help you. You'll help us, won't you, Jalen?"

There were so many reasons not to trust these agents, including this pot of mine. This pot, which in their hands, said, *We can get to you and*, worse, *we can get to your family*.

But I was so *tired*. I'd quit once already, and I still had more than half my Challenges left. I'd created a path of destruction through the streets of New Orleans, and I would need *someone* on my side when it became clear that the damage was mine. They knew more about this than I did, no thanks to Gemini, who, apparently, hadn't told me the whole truth. And these agents could get me to Nina—quickly.

But perhaps most of all, after all the guessing and second-guessing, I needed so badly to trust *someone*.

I reached out with a single finger to touch the lip of the bowl. I felt myself nod numbly. "I'll help you," I whispered.

13

The car's engine purred, Agent Griffin at the wheel. "Where we going?" he grumbled, his eyes glaring at me in the rearview mirror.

Ellie's hand tightened around mine. A warning not to tell them. She was right. I wanted to trust these agents. I thought I could. But there was no reason to tell them everything.

"Head toward the Garden District."

Agent Griffin's eyes narrowed further, a feat I would've thought impossible. "*Where* in the Garden District?"

"Just go," I said. "I'll tell you where to go when we get there."

Agent Griffin grunted and slammed the car into drive. We pulled out of the parking lot, and an arrow drove straight at my backseat window, a deadly dot that grew into a lethal line as it sliced toward me. It bounced off my window with a ting, and I flinched. Agent Cygnus shot me a look of concern.

In a few short moments, we were back at the terminal

for the Algiers Ferry. Flashing blue lights dotted and spun against the West Bank. I sank into the backseat and prayed all the people on the ferry were okay.

"What a mess," Agent Cygnus said. "Take the bridge. It's faster, anyway."

Agent Griffin sped away, and moments later we stopped at the mouth of the Crescent City Connection Bridge. We'd gotten here so fast! I'd never thought about how fast and easy cars are.

As we approached, we saw more flashing lights. Orange ones, this time. White-and-orange striped construction barrels blocked the entrance to the bridge. Agent Griffin growled and smacked the steering wheel. Agent Cygnus sighed. "Roll down your window, Steve."

"Hey!" Agent Cygnus yelled over Agent Griffin to a group of construction workers. "What gives?"

Two construction workers wearing orange reflective vests and hard hats crossed to the car. I cringed. If they were Keepers, would they still attack while we were with these agents? I thought they would.

One guy—a huge man with a bulbous red nose and overalls—hitched his radio back onto his tool belt. "Bridge is closed. Take the ferry."

"Ferry's closed, too," Agent Griffin snapped. "We supposed to swim across?"

The huge construction worker shrugged. "Stinks for you." His radio crackled, and he turned and walked back to his group. Agent Griffin pressed the button to slide his window back up.

The other construction worker—this one with mirrored sport sunglasses and dreadlocks to his waist—leaned toward the car. His hair swung down like thick rope. "Jest go round de barrels."

Agent Griffin never turned to look at him but stuck a finger in his ear and jimmied his knuckle. He jerked the gearshift down and swung the wheel.

"Hang on. I'ma go around the barrels."

We were, at last, crossing the Mississippi River. It lay below us, snaking through the city. Brennan clutched the door handle, his knuckles white. I didn't care for how high up this bridge was, either.

It was eerie, riding in the only car on this bridge. We were high enough up and far enough out to feel like the only humans on earth. I took deep breaths.

"What the—!" Agent Griffin shouted. He stomped on the brakes, and we skidded in a half circle before the back of the car dropped with a thunk. Ellie, Brennan, and I were thrown against the ceiling of the Lincoln.

A hole in the bridge. The car teetered, the front half of it still on the bridge, the back half dangling far above the Mississippi River. The front tires were still spinning, and a smoking, groaning whirr of rubber stench lifted from the two front wheels.

We were frozen, all five of us, too terrified to even

speak, for fear we would upset our balance. I snaked my eyes sideways to Brennan. His face was pulled tight like a knot. The lump in his throat bobbed. I snaked my eyes farther, toward the back window. The swirling river lay far below. My head spun with the height.

"Libra," Ellie whispered.

I didn't nod. I couldn't. But I knew she was right. This was the work of Libra, the balancing scales. If we didn't play this just right, Libra would ensure the scales tipped in the zodiac's favor.

The construction worker, the one with the dreadlocks who had advised us to go around the barrels, sauntered up.

"Bit of a jam you in, eh!" he yelled. He hitched thumbs in the armholes of his orange vest and bobbed on his toes. My anger matched the glare of his ugly vest. The agents didn't see him. This must be Libra himself.

Agent Cygnus had sneaked a hand forward. He pushed the button that slid his window down but stopped.

"These windows, they're too small," he whispered. "We can't go through them. This car would drop for sure."

Brennan made a sound like a small whimper.

The construction worker, Libra, approached the open window. He bent in half, dreadlocks swinging over the chasm in the middle of the bridge. He tsk-tsked our situation. "Watch dat first step. It's a doozy!" He threw his head back and cackled, the sun flashing off his sunglasses.

Agent Griffin and Agent Cygnus heard none of Libra's teasing, of course. Agent Griffin inched his hand off the steering wheel to his hip. He arched his back to reach for his gun. What was he thinking, drawing his gun now? The tires screamed and the car dropped an inch. Or twenty. The oxygen in the car was sucked away as we all snatched a breath.

Agent Griffin raised his gun and pointed it at the windshield. "I'll shoot it out," he grumbled. "Then we go out the front." He touched gun barrel to glass.

Brennan squeaked. "Kick back," he breathed. "Not *on* the glass. *Away* from it."

Griffin paused, then nodded and pulled the gun away from the glass a few inches.

"It'll still give some kick," Brennan said, his voice slowly steadying. "Agent Cygnus, you'll have to throw your body forward, through the window, to offset the recoil. Do it as the gun is fired to keep our balance."

Cygnus nodded slightly. "Yes, right, smart," he said. It appeared he was trying to keep his tone light. "Son, you want a job with the government?"

"No."

"Fair enough. On three, Griffin."

Griffin nodded. "One, two, *three!*"

BLAM!

The gun exploded, a blast of fire in a tiny space. My ears began ringing immediately from the shot. Cygnus crashed through the glass after the bullet. He landed on the hood of the car, sprawled head first, his feet still with us in the car, draped over the dashboard.

The car teetered and tottered, moaned and groaned, but it eventually came to rest, leaving us in the backseat bobbing a few inches lower than before. Libra stood next to Cygnus and clapped his hands slowly, loudly, clap, clap, clap.

"Nice work, Jalen and friends," he said, pacing next to our balancing act. "Nice, nice. Dese scales, dey hard to balance, no?" He raised and lowered the palms of his hands, like scales correcting themselves. As he did, the car swayed and creaked. "Jest like life. Right or wrong. Left or right. Black or white. Alive or dead."

Lost or left? It was the question that had been with me since this morning. One or the other. In Libra's world, everything was absolute. Slightly off balance was the same as crashing to the ground to a Libra.

I understood our Challenge, then: Get out of this car alive, and I win. Or don't.

Absolute.

Agent Cygnus had to be uncomfortable, sprawled across broken safety glass and gripping the hood. He could save himself now, roll to one side and the car would plummet. I held back a shudder so I wouldn't move the car even more.

"Ellie," he said over his shoulder. "You first. Climb over me."

Ellie was in the middle of the backseat, so it made sense for her to go first. She inched toward the edge of the seat, then slowly, painstakingly, lifted. The car dropped centimeters. It felt like miles.

But Ellie, this Ellie, was amazingly graceful. She patiently crouched, waiting for the car to correct itself before inching forward again. I thought of the hours-ago Ellie from before the change, the one with the subtlety of a bulldozer. Tears welled.

I closed my eyes and swallowed. Alive or dead.

I didn't care for Libra's view of the world. I was a potter after all. My sense of balance wasn't *add to this, add to that/ take from this, take from that*. Balance, to me, was a spinning, growing thing, something that I plunged my thumbs into and pinched and pulled and created and crafted. Something *I* controlled.

Ellie had oozed forward at a snail's pace and was now halfway out of the car. Brennan's breath was shallow puffs. I hoped he wouldn't hyperventilate. I hoped I wouldn't join him.

The moment Ellie's sneakers hit solid ground, she dug *The Keypers of the Zodiack* out of her messenger bag. She leaned into the open window and read.

"'Libra, the scales. August 10—September 15. Like the balancing scales that represent thee, Libra, thou art objective, a

master of harmony and balance. Thou rarely choosest sides,
preferring to shun all judgment, even to the point of crippling
thyself in the face of a decision. Thou art a peaceful pleasure
seeker who loves beauty and warmth, who loathes loneliness.
Thou art an excellent listener, but thou hast a weakness for
juicy gossip, and thou art both impressionable and manipula-
tive when it comes to spreading untruths. Know that thy sense
of justice—an eye for an eye, no doubt—leaves two blind."

"Yes, yes," the pacing Libra said, "dat's me."

Agent Cygnus turned his head to Ellie. "What is that? That book?"

Ellie looked at me, but I was too afraid to shake my head. *Don't tell him,* my instincts screamed. *Don't!*

But she held up the cover of the book. *"The Keypers of the Zodiack.* The one we used to—"

"Ellie!" I screamed. The car bobbled deeply, the front tires squealed. Brennan gulped air. She looked at me, nodded, and tucked the book away.

"Well, look at dat!" Libra said, throwing his hands wide. He leaned toward the car again. "Such passion from you, Jalen! Don't you know? Too much passion—it throws you off balance." He chuckled.

"Where did you get that book?" Cygnus demanded of Ellie. He started to squirm. The car shifted, the left side skidding a little lower than the right.

"Cygnus," Griffin hissed. "Later, okay?"

Cygnus cleared his throat. "Yes. Right. Jalen, you're next."

"No," I said. "Brennan's next." Brennan looked at me with wild eyes.

"If you don't go next," I whispered, "I don't think you'll ever get out." My head swirled with dizziness, yes, but Brennan's fear of the water far below was worse.

Brennan considered that: him, in the backseat, alone. He likely wouldn't have the guts to try to escape if he was back there by himself. He nodded. This Brennan knew his weaknesscs.

He gulped several deep breaths and inched toward the middle of the backseat. Ellie, outside, paced and bit her fingernails. "You can do it, Brennan. I know you can."

"I love you, Ellie," Brennan said. "But please. Shut up."

Libra laughed and hopped up and down. Envy flamed inside me at how easily Libra jumped and gestured and moved, while I was afraid to breathe. Fluid or frozen. This or that. Absolute.

Brennan crept into the front seat, slowly, slowly through the windshield, then finally, finally onto the bridge. Once the weight of his body left the car, the Lincoln swayed violently. Agent Griffin cursed under his breath.

The moment Brennan's feet were both solidly planted on concrete, he curled into a ball and jammed his eye sockets into his knees. Ellie dropped her messenger bag, wrapped her arms around him, and glared up at Libra. "Get them out of there," she said.

Libra crossed his muscular arms over his chest. "Dey doin' fine, girl. Jest fine."

"Who are you talking to?" Cygnus barked. Ellie chewed her lip.

"You're next, Jalen," Griffin growled from the driver's seat. "Make it quick, huh?"

Sure, right. Quick.

I lifted off the seat, slowly, telling myself do *not* look down. Virgo's heavy sapphire birthstone flopped forward in my baggy cargo pocket when I stood. I instinctively grabbed for it. My sudden movement made the car bob. I closed my eyes and took a slow, deep breath before continuing. My head felt fuzzy.

"Jalen!" a voice wailed. I opened my eyes.

My . . . *mom*? Standing beside Libra?

"Mrs. Jones?" Ellie whispered.

Yes. There was my mom, twisting and untwisting the handle of her purse. She shook, and rivers of mascara ran down her cheeks. "Mom?" I whispered.

"Jalen, I can't find him! We need him, Jalen. I have to leave you." Her voice wavered as she said this last part. *Hearing* her upset over the phone was one thing. *Seeing* her upset was another.

"Why are you here?" I asked her. I was numb. Why was she telling me this now? Why wasn't she helping me?

"What?" Agent Griffin growled at me. "Believe me, I'd rather be anyplace else."

Mom swiped at the tears on her cheeks, smearing black mascara across her skin like war paint.

Mascara? I knew then it was a trick. Another of Gemini's twin tricks. My mother never wore makeup. And I didn't think this new version of her would pause long enough to freshen her face.

"Listen to your mama, Jalen," Libra cooed. "She leaving you. Don't dat make you sad?"

My anger flared. Libra and Gemini were a team, trying to throw me off balance. They knew the best way to do that was to use my mother. The weight they'd just added to the scales was a heavy one.

I crawled between the two front seats, the car dipping and swaying the whole time. My mother—Gemini's version of my mother—sobbed and cursed as I did.

"I couldn't stay with your Nina," I heard my mom's voice say. "I left her, too." I inched forward, determined not to let her upset me. I wasn't sure I would win.

As I climbed over Agent Cygnus's feet, I raked my scalp across a screw in what remained of the rearview mirror. I whimpered. The car dipped, flinging my stomach into my mouth.

"If you'd never gotten sick," Mom's voice said, "your father would still be with us." I wanted to scream, *"Shut up!,"* but I knew if I did, the force of my anger would push this car into the chasm.

I crunched across the glass of the windshield over Agent

Cygnus's head and stepped on his finger. The whole time, I reminded myself that balance was *not* an either/or. Not to me. Life was not a series of absolutes. It was a mystery, a blissful mystery, one that can't simply be chosen. No, life must be crafted.

At last, I lowered myself onto the bridge. The moment my shoes touched concrete, my mom's twin disappeared with a wail. The weight of her sadness lifting away made me sway, because my weight was still here and still very, very heavy.

Libra applauded again, clap, clap, clap. He sauntered up to the edge of the chasm, next to the teetering Lincoln. He threw his arms wide, tilted back his head, closed his eyes.

"Push me, Jalen," he whispered. "You know you want to."

My orange anger screamed at me: *Do it!* It would feel so good, that kind of revenge. He won't get hurt—he's a Keeper. Do it! Push him!

I cracked my knuckles. This was another absolute, an eye for an eye. "No."

He chuckled, a deep, gurgling laugh, and tossed me his birthstone—an opal. He was done here. I'd lived. It didn't matter to him if Griffin and Cygnus survived.

I lifted the milky blue-white stone to the skies, but Libra surprised me, hugging me before I chanted.

"Dat's a smart girl," he whispered. "Most tings, dey not *good* or *bad*. We make dem dat way. You understand."

I nodded. I think I did. *"Sic itur ad astra."*

Libra's mirrored sunglasses morphed into shiny brass weighing platforms, his dreadlocks turned into the chains supporting them. His lithe body and muscled arms hardened into metal. He lifted into the skies, a set of scales swaying and swirling, perfectly off balance.

I shook off the experience as best I could and turned to make sure Agents Cygnus and Griffin were okay. Griffin oozed forward, trying to inch around the steering wheel. Cygnus looked over his shoulder at him, checking to see where his partner might be.

And then Cygnus rolled off the hood of the car.

The wheels screeched and the car swayed.

"Agent Griffin!" Brennan yelled.

Griffin's eyes grew wide. He scrambled up and out the shattered windshield, arms and legs flailing as the car groaned backward. The tip of his toe pushed off the falling car's front bumper. He leaped, and the front half of his body made it onto the bridge, but his legs dangled far, far, far above the river. The hum of the car's engine grew quieter. And then, a faint splash.

Ellie, Brennan, and I darted forward to drag Griffin onto the bridge. His legs pumped and kicked, and I ignored the dizzy sensation of being on the edge of the world. We pulled him safely onto the concrete.

Griffin didn't even take a moment to catch his breath or to thank us. He sprang to his feet and ran at Cygnus in tackle mode, who was thumbing through *The Keypers of the Zodiack*, eyes shining. Griffin growled and flattened Cygnus against the pavement. Griffin yanked the book out of Cygnus's hands and tossed it aside, throwing punches and swear words.

Brennan dashed forward and grabbed the book, Ellie scooped up her messenger bag, and the three of us ran.

My pounding feet drummed a realization into my pounding heart: Those agents didn't care about casting the Keepers away. They didn't care about anyone's personalities, about world peace, about destroying the stone to ensure the safety of humanity. They just wanted Ophiuchus's stone. The power that comes with the stone, the power to control death. If those Keepers were to be cast away, I would need to do it on my own.

14

We dashed away from the wreckage, heading back down the hill of the bridge, back to the same ridiculous West Bank we'd left. What an obstacle this river was! I felt like a pioneer, someone trying to navigate this "brave new world" on horseback.

And I was still shaking from Agent Cygnus nearly sending Agent Griffin to a watery grave, and from seeing my mother. It hadn't really been her, of course, but it had been so *real*. Did my mom blame me for my dad leaving? No, she was smarter than that, kinder than that. Wasn't she?

All of this made me think of that huge claw they'd used to scrape the bottom of the Gulf, searching for my dad—it stirred up some ugly, muddy things.

Gemini fell into step beside me. "I told you not to trust them."

My anger flamed. "You didn't tell me the whole truth. Ophiuchus is more powerful than you said, right?"

Gemini didn't answer my question.

"So why, then, should I listen to *you* when you tell me who to trust? How do I know you're not just another Challenge, some tricky trap or something?"

Gemini looked back over her shoulder, I assumed to check where the agents were. She grabbed my arm but didn't stop—she knew we needed to keep moving.

"Jalen, I didn't tell you the truth because I didn't know if I could trust you with that knowledge," she whispered, an edge to her voice. But it wasn't anger, I thought. It was more like . . . desperation? "A stone that can reverse death isn't exactly the kind of thing we Keepers want a lot of humans to know about."

I cracked my knuckles. She had a point. Still, the small amount of trust I'd placed in her was now a fragile thing.

By the time we reached the entry of the bridge, the construction workers were tossing the barrels into the back of a dump truck. Ellie tapped one of the workers on the shoulder.

"Those barrels need to stay," she said. "No one can drive across that bridge."

The huge man in overalls shot us a funny look. "Boss man says we're done here." He gestured at the bridge. We followed the point of his finger.

There was no hole. The expanse of the Crescent City Connection was a single, complete span. In perfect balance.

The construction worker turned to us, his look now sour. "Where'd you come from?"

"The ferry," Brennan said. He pulled our elbows. "Headed back there now."

"Jalen!" The voice came from on top of the hill, on the bridge. Agent Cygnus.

"Hey!" The construction worker in overalls marched up the bridge toward him. "What're you doing on this bridge?" He whipped out his radio and said, "Boss, looks like we got us some trouble here."

We saw our opportunity. We turned to run, back toward Algiers Point. But we only got three or four yards before we saw the convenience store worker from earlier. His head was bobbing, earbuds blaring. Capricorn had returned.

He morphed like lightning into a goat and charged us. I sidestepped, but Ellie didn't have the chance to do the same. Capricorn butted Ellie in the gut with a sickening blow. I heard the air escape her. The goat galloped away. It was still not time for Capricorn.

Brennan and I scooped Ellie up, each of us taking an arm and running. She shrugged us off once she got her breath back. She stopped.

"Capricorn!" she shouted, her fists tight balls. "Could you *be* more passive-aggressive?"

Gemini threw her head back and guffawed, her black

hair shining in the now bright sun. I reached back to take Ellie's hand. But I didn't know whose hand to grab.

Two Ellies. Again.

I wished more than ever I knew which Ellie was which, although it was probably good I *didn't* know which one could morph into my family members. No telling what the orange inside might make me do if I *did* know.

So instead, I sighed. "Gemini, your twin is a real piece of work."

✳ ✳ ✳

Because we didn't know where else to go, we headed back to Algiers Point. "Least it's daytime now," Brennan said, pointing at the bright sun. Yes, daytime. It was at least 11 a.m. I held in a few cuss words.

The skies now shouted a loud winter blue. Those skies! They looked so cheery, so friendly in the daylight. All that sunshine, all that blue, hiding all those starry secrets. What a lie, blue skies! At least the nighttime sky tells the truth.

Just as the orange inside me started rising, I heard it: *PSSSSSHHHHTTT!*

A rainbow-colored hot-air balloon kissed the top of a nearby grove of trees, then rose higher against that lying sky. It had just lifted off.

Brennan and I exchanged a look. He grinned and

nodded. I nodded back, but bit my lip. Those things flew so high. Could I do it?

The Ellies must've *felt* our plan formulating. One of them dropped the hand that had been shading her eyes.

"No. Unh-uh." One Ellie spoke up. "No hot-air balloons. Are y'all insane?"

But the other Ellie glared at her. "Do you have a better idea how we're going to cross that river?"

The first Ellie blinked, then turned to me. "A hot-air balloon? Jalen, you can't be serious. You shook like a leaf just climbing the stairs of the ferry. You really think you could handle a hot-air balloon?"

My forehead wrinkled. I could easily be talked out of this plan.

But the second Ellie took a step forward. She was face-to-face with her twin. "What is it with you, always trying to sabotage Jalen's plans?"

Ellie One shook her head slightly. "No, I—"

"Because if I was Jalen, I'd be thinking you were a Keeper about right now," Ellie Two said.

Ellie One's hands shot out. She shoved her twin so hard, Ellie Two stumbled backward onto the sidewalk. The downed Ellie looked at her bleeding palms, at the tiny bits of gravel imbedded in them, tears pooling in her eyes.

Brennan stepped between the two of them. "Cut it out! This only makes it worse."

My eyes darted between the Ellie who still stood and the Ellie who had fallen. A guess burbled through my brain as to who was who, but it was still just that: a guess.

* * *

The balloon launching pad was farther away than I thought it'd be; we ran another mile or so before we found it tucked between two warehouses. It looked like a huge parking lot. If it weren't for a tiny woman in a drab olive jumpsuit struggling with a hot-air balloon basket, we would've missed it altogether.

The woman grunted and pushed the heavy basket, sweat dripping off her face, swear words dripping off her lips. Her hair was bright white, her skin tight but wrinkled. She had to be sixty, maybe even seventy years old.

An Ellie stopped cold. "Her? No way. She's a Keeper for sure. C'mon, guys—"

"You wanna rent a balloon?"

We spun around to a massive guy with hair every-where—a beard, shaggy mop hair, a single bushy eyebrow. Hair peeked out of his shirt collar and poked out of his knuckles. He grinned, and a toothpick punctuated his smile like an exclamation point. I thought of a huge teddy bear.

"You kids interested in a balloon ride?" he repeated.

Ellie swallowed. "Yes," Brennan said. "You work here?"

"Proud owner for almost twenty years," he said.

We walked toward the basket attached to the base of the balloon. Over the open basket was a metal framework that held a fan, which filled the balloon with air, and a flame, which made the balloon rise. I remembered studying weather balloons in science class. Weather balloons had those same gadgets.

The woman in the jumpsuit grunted and shoved the basket over on its side, with the wire framework jutting out to the left. She began unfurling a New Orleans Saints balloon on the ground. The woman prepped the balloon, cussing and kicking fabric the whole time. She turned and spit on the ground. One of the Ellies grabbed my hand.

The woman. She looked so irate, so intense, so . . . *imperfect*, like a human. If she was human, I wondered what she'd been like before: Had she been a delicate, polite person who sipped her tea, pinkie out? Or is she the same person now as she was then, and now just expresses her feelings differently? What parts of us are changeable, and what parts of us are simply us?

I looked for Gemini, but she had again disappeared. If she were gone, then a Keeper was likely nearby. I stiffened.

The owner must've seen us staring at the old woman. "That's Sylvie," he said, lifting his bearded chin at her. She flicked on the fan attached over the basket. The balloon on the ground started quivering to life, puffing full of air.

"Your mom?" Brennan asked.

The man chuckled. "I'd know a few more cuss words if she was."

The Ellies and Brennan laughed.

"Naw, Sylvie's had a hard life," the man said. He shifted the toothpick to the other side of his mouth with his jaw. "Got a son she never talks to. Truth is, we don't pick our family. Some of us'd be better off if we could." He shook his head.

As we got closer to the balloon, a cell phone rang. I jumped at the sound. The scrap of a woman unfurling the balloon ripped open a pocket on her jumpsuit and jabbed a button. "Yeah?"

An Ellie shivered. "Guys . . ." she warned in a whisper.

The expression on the woman's face changed from sour apple to applesauce as she listened over the next minute or so. "But Chuck's okay? I mean, everyone on the ferry's okay, right?"

She marched toward us, but the intensity of her knit eyebrows made it too difficult to see if her eyes were Keeper black. The closer she got to us, the hotter I burned with alert. I stood straighter.

But she passed us by. She crossed to a silver pickup truck, hopped inside, and sped away.

"Well, I'll be," the hulking hairy man said. He spit the toothpick on the ground. "Chuck's her son. Never thought I'd see the day."

"You can say that again," Brennan muttered. I elbowed

him but smiled. Looks like I had made a happy lapse in judgment. My shoulders fell. I felt my armor coming off.

And I actually smiled a little. Because Sylvie proved that maybe some good was springing out of these changes, too. Maybe some families were out there reuniting, some marriages repairing, because of me.

Maybe even my mom and dad? If she found him?

If she did find him, if they reunited . . . how could I ever change them back?

"Families," the owner said, echoing my thoughts. Out of the corner of my eye, I saw him poke another toothpick into his mouth. "So many secrets."

The way he said it make my skin prickle. I looked at him. He was staring at me, two beady black eyes in his face of fur.

"I know the truth about your father, Jalen," he said. "I know what really happened."

Had he said it? I shook my head. No. But I moved closer to him, as if I expected that the truth could only be told in a whisper.

"You want to know what happened, don't you, Jalen?" The toothpick stabbed the air between us. "You want to know the truth."

No. I wasn't ready to know for sure. Not when my hope that he *might* be alive was flickering again. "No." A step closer.

"Yes, you do." The owner's hairy face no longer looked

like a teddy bear. He was now a grizzly, his soft furry face now a mass of sharp pointed whiskers. He grabbed my arm with his strong hand.

"No!" I tried to shake loose.

The owner threw his head back and growled. He shrank into mist, his hand on my arm burning like acid. The massive hairy person withered to a tiny hard black spot gripping my arm, whiskers transforming into buggy legs. The toothpick stretched, hardened, curled, its point now bearing a nasty stinger. The smelly vapors disappeared, leaving behind a single scorpion. I screamed and flung the creature off my arm to the ground.

"Scorpio!" an Ellie screamed, leaping back. "It's—"

I stomped squarely down on the scorpion with a single *oomph*. Scorpion guts oozed onto the pavement, and its jointed, curved tail twitched.

The four of us inched forward, huddling over the dead creature.

"That's it?" Brennan asked. "That's all?"

We waited for the birthstone, another sign, *something*. But there was nothing. One of the Ellies shrugged and pulled out her copy of *The Keypers of the Zodiack* and read:

" 'Scorpio, the scorpion. November 23–November 29. Scorpio, thou art a mystery; secrets, magic, and taboos haunt thee to thy core. Others are drawn to thee for thine intensity, *thy piercing intellect. Thy generosity and confidence make thee a loyal friend. Thou art on a quest for self-improvement, under which lies a nasty competitive streak and a lust for power. Relentless, thou art, and thy insensitivity makes many an enemy. No one can pierce another's soul to the degree that thou art capable. Such power might be passion, might be possession. Honesty is a weapon to thee, as thou cravest truth at all cost. Thy cunning, suspicious nature leads to much brooding, but ultimately, thy wary temperament serves thee well. Thou art a master of persuasion, Scorpio. Know that thy fire to succeed can be either a triumph or a downfall.' "*

"Honesty is a weapon," I thought with a smirk. Scorpio did know the fate of my father. The truth was his poison. He'd drawn me near so his sting would be fatal.

I leaned over the scorpion guts smeared across the pavement. "Low blow, Scorpio."

It was like I'd taunted the thing, because BOOM!, the scorpion's guts exploded. Waves of scorpions—hundreds and hundreds of them—scurried out of the dead scorpion's shell like it was a bottomless pit.

And this swarm was on a mission. They jerked and clicked toward us, shells shimmering, tails twitching.

"On the basket!" an Ellie shouted. "Up!"

We clamored on top of the empty basket, which was still lying on its side. But the weight of the four of us on the side of the basket caused the wicker to buckle. And because it was woven, the scorpions could climb it. Their torturous tails inched closer, jerking, jointed tails like the vertebrates in a spine.

We could outrun them, sure, but I'd come to realize throughout these Challenges that I had to *defeat* them, not just outlast them. But it was obvious that we didn't have time to come up with a plan here.

The side of the basket sunk lower and lower, the scorpions climbed higher and higher. We had to jump off and regroup somewhere else.

"One at a time," Brennan was saying. He'd come to the same conclusion. He pointed to a spot about three feet away where the swarm dwindled. "Jump there."

One of the Ellies went first. The force of her legs springing off the basket caused the basket to buckle further. She was in the clear, running for a warehouse. But the drooping basket gave the scorpions an advantage. Two or three of the larger insects trickled over the top where Brennan, the other Ellie, and I teetered. We stomped and swiped at them, but with each motion, the basket wobbled, threatening to topple us into the nest of scorpions below.

The other Ellie jumped and made it into a clearing. I shivered. The crabs had been sharp and slimy, the other animals of the zodiac, ferocious. But facing thousands of stinging creatures nearly unglued me. They were just so . . . *buggy*.

"You go next!" I shouted over the din of a thousand creatures. Brennan shook his head. I glared at him and pointed at a clearing just a few feet away. "Go!"

Brennan rolled his eyes but leaped. The basket crunched under the force, the side sunk lower still. I could now hear the balloon's fan beside me as it chewed up scorpions and spit them out. *Thank you, fan,* I thought as I swiped away another bug.

At least, with scorpions, you knew when they were about to attack. They grab you with their nasty insect arms, arch their tails over their heads, and take aim before they strike. This courtesy allowed me to spot and flick away the ones ready to strike before swiping away the others.

The balloon attached to the basket was now puffed with cool air from the fan, but scorpions were moving inside it quickly, trying to crawl up the slick interior fabric. I knew from the experiment we did with weather balloons that this balloon wouldn't rise with just the cool air filling it. It needed hot air from the flame to rise.

The flame! It had not yet been lit. But to light it from here, I'd have to lie down on the side of the basket and stretch above its opening, allowing myself to be covered in scorpions in the process. I spasmed with shivers.

It would work, though, I knew it. I eased down to my knees, then onto my belly. Virgo's birthstone wedged uncomfortably under my leg, and I scowled thinking of it, still here in my pocket. A scorpion sprang into my hair. I about lost it before pinching it dead.

"What are you doing?" Brennan yelled from across the launch pad.

First, I guessed I had to turn *off* the fan, or the balloon would rise when I turned on the gas. I didn't want that.

I wanted a flame thrower.

I leaned over the edge of the basket, took a deep breath, and plunged my right hand into the swarm of scorpions to turn off the fan. The back of my hand felt like it had been stabbed with a hot needle, and it immediately began to hum with pain. I had been stung.

Fan off. The balloon began to wilt, and the many scorpions trapped inside made the collapsed fabric jump and pop. The gas nozzle was next to the fan. I reached for it with the same hand and tried to turn the nozzle like a faucet, but pain from the poison made my hand so numb it was useless. I took another breath, swiped an arched scorpion off my shirt, and plunged my left hand in toward the gas nozzle. My left wrist was stung as I turned on the heat.

A blue flame shot up with a hiss, then morphed into orange-yellow fire. The kind of fire that signals power. Scorpions screamed and sizzled, melting under the heat.

I scrambled to my feet and jumped to the closest clearing, but not before my ankle got pierced by a scorpion sting, too. My hands were both numb, but I managed to push the heavy basket in a circle, torching every shiny, nasty bug in sight. I think I was screaming, too. Because really, torching scorpions calls for it.

Brennan saw what I was doing and raced *back* through the swarm of scorpions to help me aim the fire by rotating the thick basket. Within minutes, the scorpions were nothing but a pile of cinders. A light breeze lifted some ash up and away. I didn't even see the black snakestone birthstone poking out of the coals; an Ellie pointed it out to me.

The stone was hot to the touch, but after a few minutes, I could lift it and chant. I was afraid I'd drop it, my hands were so numb, but the charred remains of Scorpio illuminated and crawled into the sky.

"You get stung?" I asked Brennan. My tongue felt like it was three feet thick.

He smiled. "Three or four times, I guess." His words were mushy, too. I smiled back.

"Thanks, Brennan," I said, wrinkling my nose at the sound of my words.

Instead of answering, he winked. I was surprised to feel a tingle like a shooting star.

It's the stings, I told myself. *The stings.*

✳ ✳ ✳

"Good news," the Ellie who had run into the warehouse said. She stepped over the charred remains of the Saints balloon. "There's another balloon in the shed."

We dragged it out. Well, Brennan and the Ellies dragged

it. I pushed with the limp mitts my hands had become. Brennan shuffled and every once in a while had to stop and feverishly scratch the places where he'd been stung.

We laid the basket on its side and unfolded the balloon, just like the lady in the jumpsuit had done. This balloon was dusty, and flipping it around the lot made the Ellies sneeze—both tiny, delicate sneezes that sounded like *ch!*, so different from the honking blast of a sneeze that Ellie had once had.

The balloon was decorated with a giant skull and cross-bones. One of the Ellies placed a hand on her hip when she saw that. "Really?" she asked. Brennan chuckled.

The fan clicked on and filled the balloon. As it puffed to life, I thought out loud: "How are we going to pay for this?" One of the Ellies smirked at me. I dropped my shoulders at her glare. "I mean, we can't just *steal* this thing."

"Use that birthstone," the Ellie said. She pointed to my cargo pants pocket. "I told you, that thing's worth gobs of money."

Brennan shook his head and dashed into the warehouse. When he returned, we righted the basket and climbed aboard. "What did you do in there?" I asked, more to take my mind off the flight than anything else.

He shrugged. "Left Sylvie my credit card."

Those darn stings. Tingling again.

The four of us crowded into the basket. It was cozy, like

standing in a large bathroom stall together. I thanked our lucky stars (lucky stars—*right)* that Gemini could come and go as she pleased. This basket would be very tight with her. As I thought it, a wind lifted from below, poofing our hair, the balloon—telling us, I think, that Gemini was never far.

The balloon was ready. I swallowed. My throat felt like it was closing. I didn't know whether it was from the scorpion stings or the heights I was about to face.

An Ellie's hand was on the gas nozzle. "Ready, Jalen?"

Wow—I must've *looked* terrified, too. I took a shaky breath. "Sure," I said, but my voice squeaked, my tongue still numb.

The instant the gas *heeshed*, I felt like I was going to throw up. I sat on the floor of the basket and looked at two pairs of Ellie knees and a set of Brennan knees. The sensation of going up and up and up made my eyesight black out to a tiny pinpoint of light.

"How is this not freaking you out?" I asked Brennan.

He pointed down and grinned. "It's the water that freaks me out. Not the height. See how *veeeery* far away the water is from here?"

"Really?" I asked.

He gulped. "Sorry."

An Ellie rubbed my back. "We'll get there, Jalen. We'll get there."

The swaying of the basket, the warmth of the gas flame

overhead, the rubbing of my back. It was silent. I lifted my chin and stood.

And I could see for miles. The Mississippi River arched below, as curvy as its name implies. The West Bank was now far behind us, and the twinkling, glittering lights of downtown New Orleans, already flickering in the afternoon sun, lay ahead.

"I'm coming, Nina," I whispered. "Please, hang on."

My words were whisked away by the wind.

15

What you *don't* know before you hijack a hot-air balloon is that you can't steer the thing. You are carried on the whims of the winds. You can go higher and lower, depending on how much hot air you pump into the balloon, but you must go where the heavens decide to take you.

Much like my entire day.

The gusts carried us over the river, thankfully, but they pushed us north. Nina's hospital lay much farther west. Brennan tried easing the gas valve shut a bit, and we plummeted. He opened the valve again and we soared. I wasn't sure which sensation I hated more.

If we didn't figure out how to land this thing soon, we'd be so far north, we'd be near Lake Pontchartrain. Way out of our way, with much time lost.

One of the Ellies huffed. "Let me try it," she said. She nudged Brennan aside. But before she even turned the nozzle, we heard a whistle and we started to plunge.

"I didn't even touch it!" Ellie said.

Brennan shook his head and pointed into the balloon, crumpling over our heads. "You didn't. Look."

An arrow had punctured our balloon.

A black tip of arrow, lodged way up inside our balloon. It was so tiny but so deadly. One little pinprick for our balloon to pop! I cursed myself. I led my friends into a balloon after arrows had been fired at us for hours. What was I thinking?

"Get down!" I yelled, dragging Brennan and one of the Ellie's shirts down with me. And we were dropping, dropping, dropping . . . My heart thumped in my throat when I thought of our landing. Because we were crouching, I had no idea when we'd hit. Every second was excruciating, thinking *this* might be the second we smashed into the ground. No *this* second. *This* one. *This* one . . .

Brennan tugged out of my grip, stood, and reached up. He blasted the flame full force. An arrow zipped toward him, lodging in the crook of his shirt, under his arm. His eyes widened. He drooped to the floor of the basket. He'd slowed our freefall, but had he been hit?

An Ellie pulled him toward her and slowly extracted the arrow. No blood. She peered through the hole in his clothes. A perfectly clean slice through the armpit of his shirt, but no hit.

"Sagittarius, the archer." An Ellie tapped her messenger

bag where *The Keypers of the Zodiack* was stowed. All this time we'd had arrows zipping past us, and I'd not once looked at the Sagittarius horoscope. Avoiding Sagittarius, my old sign, was something I was good at.

We kept plummeting fast, fast enough for my T-shirt to billow out with air from below. We fell and we fell and we fell. My new worst nightmare. And it was compliments of my original horoscope sign.

The basket crashed into the ground. The wicker crumpled like paper. The four of us were thrown out of the basket like a game dice from a cup. My arms and legs flew wildly. My head slammed against a cold slab of marble.

I wasn't knocked out, but I was dizzy and disoriented. One of the Ellies pulled me behind a mausoleum.

We'd crash-landed in a cemetery, and by the looks of it, the Saint Louis Cemetery No. 1. Some of the bodies buried here saw the Civil War; some, the American Revolution. In a city below sea level, like New Orleans, the graves aren't underground. They're in mausoleums, row upon row of stone altars and chapels, tiny concrete homes for the dead. It's not a graveyard, with trees and grass and things that are living to offset the things that are dead. No, this cemetery was fully concrete and stone—ground, walls, statues, all of it. All of it, the color of bones.

I blinked, my vision wavering over the angels and gargoyles and saints that cast stretchy shadows in the late-afternoon sun. The wrought-iron fences (gates to keep in the dead?) around many of the graves were rusting. The concrete on many of the mausoleums was crumbling. This was where things came to decay.

Where we hid, candles flickered in colorful rows and fresh flowers were stacked neatly at the foot of the grave. Someone had been here, recently, mourning their loss. My throbbing head flickered momentarily to Nina. *No,* I scolded myself. *I won't think of her here.*

"Do you think Sagittarius is here, too?" Ellie whispered. I nodded.

Brennan wasn't with us. I was too scared to call out his name, scared that a loaded bow was pulled taut just inches away, around the corner of this grave. But I was also afraid that he'd been hurt much worse than I had when we'd landed.

Two or three graves down, a pebble *plipped* into the aisle between the tombs. Then another.

Brennan! I picked up a pebble and tossed it, too. We waited, wondering if he'd seen it. In a heartbeat, he jumped into the aisle and streaked toward us, leaping over us, diving onto the rocky earth behind us.

An arrow chased him, zipping by us so close it snuffed out the flames on the candles. I shivered at the thin trail of smoke left behind, showing me exactly how quickly a flame can be extinguished.

The arrow had whizzed directly down our row.

Sagittarius was near, maybe four or five graves north. We had to move, and quickly.

We scraped and skidded in the gravel around the corner of the mausoleum. An arrow bounced off the peeling concrete behind us, its honed point crumbling the gravestones even further.

Our chests heaved with lost breath. Ellie pulled *The Keypers of the Zodiack* from her messenger bag. "Sagittarius, Sagittarius . . ." she whispered. "Here!"

Ellie lifted the book into a faint stream of sunlight to better see.

> " 'Sagittarius, the archer. December 18—January 18. Sagittarius, like the arrows thou firest so keenly, thou art straightforward and swift, searching for answers with restless impatience. Logic and wit are two of thy sharpest weapons, and thou canst fire them with reckless extravagance. Despite the hasty launching of thine arsenal, thou rarely missest thy target, hunting with an intuitive accuracy others find both miraculous and disturbing. Overcome thy carelessness, and thou wilt never miss. Compassion and loyalty affect thine aim."

Zip! An arrow pierced the cover of the book, the razor-sharp tip stopping mere inches from the space between Ellie's eyes. Ellie blinked, then slumped against the mausoleum like she *had* been struck.

The orange inside blazed into an inferno. My fists balled.

But my gut was telling me to tamp my anger down, that something was off. Sagittarius had been given many opportunities to strike. So many near misses. So many almosts.

"These are warning shots," I heard myself say out loud. "Sagittarius could hit us if that was the goal. No, this sign is trying to tell us something."

Brennan was shaking his head as I spoke. I turned to him. "I know, okay? This used to be my sign. Trust me."

At that, I knew my plan. I stood and stepped from behind the tombstone.

I opened my arms wide. "Go ahead!" I yelled, my eyes squeezed shut. "Shoot me!" My heart thrummed. Was I nuts?

"You know I won't abuse Ophiuchus's powers!" I yelled, spinning now, arms still wide. I managed to open my eyes, more to check that I was still alive and whole than to show any amount of bravery. I felt like I *was* my heartbeat standing there, so stripped down, so vulnerable. In the next moment, I would either continue to be or I would cease to be. Just like every corpse in this cemetery. Each one, a heartbeat, *beat, beat, beat* . . . snuffed.

Nothing. No arrows, thankfully, but no surrender, either. I hadn't figured it out yet.

My mind whirred back to each time we'd seen the arrows in the past. I'd been confused at first, thinking the arrows had been fired by Agents Cygnus and Griffin. We'd seen the arrows at my house. At the bulldozer. In the agents' car . . .

Every time we'd seen the agents.

"The agents!" I yelled, still spinning.

"Ah, very good, Jalen," someone whispered. Her voice was ice on my skin. I whipped around. A ghost of a woman disappeared behind a mausoleum. I saw nothing but the wisp of a braid and the hem of a dress. I ran to catch up, but when I peeked around the corner, no one was there. I shivered.

"What do we need to know about the agents?" I asked, still leaning around the corner of the grave. "Should we trust them?"

An arrow whizzed through the inches-wide space between my face and my hands, the side of the arrowhead grazing my knuckles and slicing them like a knife. I stuck a knuckle in my mouth and tasted metallic blood. I turned in the direction of the arrow. Where I looked, a shadow flitted across the face of a saint, making the statue look like it was mumbling prayers.

"I take it that's a no."

"Believe me, Jalen," the icy voice whispered. From where? I couldn't tell. "Believe me, you can't trust them."

I felt myself scowl. This was just like Sagittarius. I had a lifetime of Sagittarian predictions and suggestions and forecasts that didn't make sense. "Fine. I won't trust them," I scoffed.

"No! You've *never* believed me, Jalen!" Then I heard it: the unmistakable *wheeeez* of an arrow flying toward me. I cringed and my every muscle seized, preparing for pain. I had made the wrong choice, being so flippant with a Keeper. With Sagittarius.

But the arrow arced and skidded in the gravel, coming to rest with the arrowhead pointing at a huge mausoleum. The monument's iron gate creaked open, and a boulder blocking the entrance slid aside with a groan.

"Show me you believe me." Sagittarius's voice now echoed from inside the grave. I swallowed and took a step forward.

No. It was a trap, wasn't it? If I went inside that grave, the stone would slide back into place, and Brennan and Ellie wouldn't even hear my screams.

"Show me you believe me, Jalen. Show me you don't trust those men."

Another step forward, but I looked back over my shoulder. Where were Brennan and Ellie?

But I knew why they weren't here. Sagittarius, I'd have to face alone.

I nodded, breathed, and walked through the rusty gate of the mausoleum. It swung shut behind me. I jumped.

"Jalen," the voice echoed.

If nothing else, I had to *see* her. All the other Keepers were so blatant. All but this one. This one had always been so slippery. I squeezed through the chilly rock opening.

Inside the mausoleum, five mossy steps led down to a small open area. The grave itself was a concrete slab crumbling into dust. Ashes to ashes, dust to dust. Cobwebs clogged every cranny. The only light was the shaft of sunlight coming in through the opening I'd crawled through. It smelled earthy, moldy, like decaying leaves. Decaying *something.* My pounding heartbeat filled the chamber, or at least it seemed that way.

The movement of a shadow to the left made me jump. Dust crumbled and sprinkled to the ground. A glimmering something was there, reflecting the tiny bit of light that had stolen into this grave.

I padded down the slimy steps and moved closer. It was a mirror, an antique piece of glass with black, spidery lines etched across it and a yellowy tinge to its surface. My Nina had once told me that voodoo priestesses and practitioners were often buried with mirrors to help them navigate the spirit world. Mirrors allowed them to watch the spirits that were too beastly to look at directly.

I approached the mirror, drawn to it. What I saw snatched my breath away.

It was me. Frowning, sorrowful, Sagittarian me. With a bright pink streak blazing through my black hair.

I felt the presence move up behind me, but it didn't cast a reflection in the mirror. I couldn't take my eyes off the sad girl there.

"Do you believe in me, Jalen?" the voice asked.

I knew what she was really asking. Do I believe in *me*? The me I was going back to, the Sagittarian me.

I reached out to touch the girl in the mirror. She reached out to touch me. I liked being fiery and electric and alive. I wasn't ready to go back, wasn't ready to *be* her again. But I knew I had to. I had to sacrifice my better self to right all these wrongs. I had to trust that the Sagittarian me could be strong and brave and happy, too.

"Yes," I whispered. "I believe in you."

I touched the girl in the mirror, cold and glassy. The mirror slid off the wall, crashing into seven or eight large shards. I dug them out of the dirt and blew the dust off them, but the broken pieces of glass threw back the reflection of After Jalen. Before Jalen had disappeared into the shadows of this grave. My eyes prickled with tears.

I turned, but Sagittarius was no longer there.

An arrow shaft wobbled oddly where she had stood. Strapped to the shaft with a leather cord was a speckled deep-blue stone, a turquoise the color of painted pottery.

Her birthstone. Her surrender.

My heart slowed, and the flame inside me cooled. I blinked back my tears. I spun and searched, but there was no sign of the archer herself.

I untied the birthstone and crept out of the dark depths of the grave. Once I hit sunlight, I lifted the turquoise above my head. *"Sic itur ad astra."* Several rows down, between two lofty mausoleums, the sparkling shimmers lifted and formed a dazzling archer racing into the sky. I dashed toward it, trying to get a glimpse of her, but by the time I skidded to a halt in the gravel, Sagittarius was gone.

As elusive to me now as she'd always been.

✳ ✳ ✳

"I think we should head into the French Quarter," Brennan said. We strolled out of the cemetery like four tourists. Four tired, dirty tourists. "We can catch the streetcar on Canal and take it to the Garden District. That'll get us to the hospital."

One of the Ellies shook her blond ponytail the moment she heard "streetcar." "I don't like it," she said.

"You don't like *anything*," the other Ellie grumbled. I sighed and grabbed one of the Ellie's hand, then huffed and grabbed the other one's hand, too. We kept walking.

"El," I said to the upset Ellie. "We can jump out any-time."

"Like a ferry," Brennan said and chuckled. I laughed, too.

But one Ellie had her eyes cast down to the sidewalk, the other Ellie had a deep crinkle in her forehead. I squeezed both hands. "Ellie," I said, unsure of who exactly I was talk-ing to—my friend or her twin.

"It's okay to be afraid. But you can't let it stop you."

I smiled and touched the spot where I'd once had a pink streak of hair. I sounded a lot like old Ellie—the before-the-change Ellie who supported me after Daddy had disappeared.

Funny how our roles had switched. I missed *my* Ellie so much it hurt. I wanted *her* back. Gemini was now here, walking beside us.

The clock at Saint Louis Cathedral struck the quarter hour; it was five fifteen p.m. We had just over three hours to get to my Nina. Three hours to find Ophiuchus. Three hours to battle four more Keepers. I was just beginning to think that three hours might be enough time to get to Touro Infirmary when a shiny new black car slid around the corner.

16

We ran in the direction that we thought would lead us into the French Quarter, hoping we'd lose the black car in the swarm of tourists and one-way streets. Today was a good day to get lost in a crowd. People clogged the sidewalks, many of them wearing feathery masks or grotesque masks and piles upon piles of plastic beads, though Mardi Gras was still months away. They were singing and hugging and chanting. I ran smack into the chest of a man wearing the face of a gargoyle.

"Hey, watch it, kid," he growled from behind the plastic mask. I shivered. *Any one of these people could be a Keeper,* I thought. *They could attack at any moment.*

I looked over my shoulder but couldn't see if the new car was still behind us. Ahead, just up the street, a man was covered head to toe in silver paint and silver clothing, standing perfectly still on a platform, like a statue. One woman hovered in her shop's entryway, smacking the doorframe with a burning incense brush to ward off evil spirits. She looked at us with knowing eyes. Were they Keepers, either one?

My mind leaped to Beausoleil/Fâchénuit. We were just a block from the shop where this had all started. One of the Ellies looked at me; was she thinking about the shop, too? If so, then *that* one was my Ellie, I was sure of it. I waited to see if she'd make the suggestion. This could be it . . .

"Maybe Madame Beausoleil can help us," Brennan cut in. Rats. Another opportunity lost. My shoulders drooped.

We ducked through an alley and ran down half a block— this block was far less crowded—to the door we'd passed through just hours before.

It was boarded up. Spray-painted, too, with black paint. GO ON! GIT! the paint read in hasty, dripping letters. I could hear Madame Beausoleil saying it, shooing us with her fingertips, scooting us along just like she used to dismiss my curious dad.

I blinked. "She closed her shop?"

The thick purple curtains covering the store windows wavered. Someone was inside, peeking at us. I pounded on the door.

"Let us in, Madame Beausoleil! We need your help!" I yelled. Brennan and Ellie and Ellie pounded and yelled, too.

The black car passed this street half a block up, then must've stopped and reversed. The tires squealed. They drove straight toward us.

I saw red. I kicked the boarded-up door, hard, before chasing Brennan and the Ellies through another alley and down the next street.

* * *

We ran through the heart of the French Quarter. Virgo's birthstone was now leaving what must be a nice purple bruise on my leg, thanks to it thumping against my thigh all afternoon. Jazz music blasted out of every darkened doorway, and the smells of Cajun food blasted out behind it. The sidewalks were sticky and crowded. Tourists were flinging plastic beads up to people leaning too far over the railings of second-story wrought-iron balconies. Taurus would love this place.

I used to think of Bourbon Street as this seedy, strange part of town. But seeing it lit up now, with hundreds of neon lights flashing in the pre-dusk, it looked magical, mysterious, a place where adventures happen.

In one of the darkened doorways, I saw a purple bridesmaid's dress, a black-and-white tuxedo. William—Virgo's groom! His shoulders sagged, but the lovely bridesmaid tilted up his chin with her thumb and nodded at him earnestly. Whatever she said to him made him grin, and one corner of his mouth tugged up. He would be just fine.

A shrill whistle made me skid to a halt and look around. The cashier from the vanishing convenience store. Capricorn removed his thumb and pinkie from between his lips. He sat at an outdoor table, a red-and-white umbrella shading him from the other diners at the oyster house. His table was over-flowing with food—crawdad, shrimp, gumbo, jambalaya, oysters. He plucked an earbud from his ear and motioned for me to sit across from him.

I did. The sight of all that greasy, spicy food made my stomach flop. Which was odd, because before, I *loved* Cajun food. Loved the spice, the heat. Now, I guess, I had more than enough spice and heat on my own. Now, the smell of those boiled crawdad, those shucked oysters—a heavy, salty, fishy smell—made my lips curl.

"Eat," Capricorn said. He pinched a red crawdad and tore off its tiny, lobsterlike head. Then he popped the spine of the mudbug in two or three places, ripped off the tail, and tossed the flubbery meat into his mouth. And to finish off this nasty little feast, Capricorn lifted the head of the crawdad to his lips and sucked out its juicy brain.

My whole body contorted. "It's an eating challenge, is that it?" I asked. There had to be sixty-some-odd crawdads on this table. There was no way I could eat thirty of these bottom suckers. No. Way. I felt my head shaking.

An Ellie dropped into the chair next to me and handed over *The Keypers of the Zodiack*, already opened to our dear friend Capricorn's page. I read.

"*'Capricorn, the goat. January 19—February 15. Capricorn, what a determined loner thou art, seeking answers from the far stretches of the universe. Thou art practical and ambitious, and thy determination to uncover life's great mysteries means thou art blessed with a great deal of patience and creativity. Thy self-sufficient nature, however, appears to many as conceit. Beware thine own intolerance, as these seeds bring forth callous, petty fruit. Thou art quite aware of thy limitations, however; both thine own and others'. This awareness breeds a calm confidence, disrupted only intermittently, and usually through an aura of pandemonium. Thy disdain for chaos is paralyzing.' "*

Across the table from me, sure enough, Capricorn's crawdads were stacked on his plate in a tidy pyramid. And unlike the other diners at this oyster house, when Capricorn had stripped the shell off the crawfish meat, he carefully lined up both head and tail in the cardboard box resting at his feet. Tiny armies of empty shells.

Capricorn kept one earbud in at all times. The other, dangling earbud blasted shrill guitar music. A big contrast from the brassy blasts of trombone that boomed from inside the restaurant.

I picked up a crawdad, yanked off its head and tail, and gulped down the meat like I was swallowing a pill, before I could taste the salt, before I could feel the spongy meat on my tongue. My stomach seized all the way up to my lips, which burned like fire from all the spices cooked inside that tiny thing. I tossed the head and shell into Capricorn's box.

He lowered his eyelids at me, then straightened my shell inside the box, aligning it with the other exoskeletons. I gulped water and reached for the next crawdad with a shaky hand.

Half of Capricorn's face lifted in a snarky grin. "You don't like crawfish boils, Jalen?"

I shrugged one shoulder, but I wasn't fooling anyone. Those crawdads stared at me with beady black eyes, their thready antennae twitching in the breeze. So buggy. So like . . . like . . . *scorpions*. My stomach lurched, remembering Scorpio, remembering all those bugs.

"Maybe you'd enjoy some oysters instead?" Capricorn slid a platter across the table. The shucked oysters on it jiggled. Twelve oysters on the halfshell. Gray blobs that looked like something someone had sneezed up. I had to seal off my nose and throat to keep from vomiting. But I knew what he meant: I was expected to eat them, too.

I ripped apart another crawdad and shoved it down my throat. I tossed the shell into the box, then watched Capricorn line it up with the others.

After a few more crawdads, the oysters were losing their sheen, turning into twelve gelatinous globs. I had to turn my attention to them before they became inedible.

Saltine cracker, smear of oyster, splashes of Tabasco. Swallow. Ignore the sensation of gulping down a supersize slug. Stomach rebellion. Repeat.

I felt my skin turn green. My saliva went sour. It took every bit of my willpower to keep this food down.

After much gagging, the dozen oysters were gone, their craggy gray shells stacked neatly inside Capricorn's disposal box. I went back to the crawdads, my orange anger growing, a fire stoked by spices and disgust. Sweat dripped into my eyes, stinging them.

Sweat? This was new, too. Before, I never sweated. Too much ice inside, I supposed. I reached up to wipe the sweat away, but Brennan caught my wrist.

"Don't," he said. "That spice on your fingers will hurt like the devil if it gets in your eyes." I nodded and blinked back the sting, wiping my eyes with my forearm instead.

Capricorn had, by this point, finished his share of crawfish and oysters. His eyes shifted, making sure that no one else here really could see him. Then he lifted the messy paper plate to his mouth and began chewing it.

Uck! *Goats.* My nose wrinkled.

I cracked open and sucked down a few more crawdads. Every time I tossed a shell into the cardboard box, Capricorn lined it up properly. It was unnerving.

Shells in a box? I thought. *That's what he calls chaos?* I gagged down another mudbug. My stomach bulged. The empty shell I tossed flopped into the box. Capricorn huffed and righted it. My orange anger burbled over.

"You have no idea what real chaos is," I said to Capricorn. He smirked and started nibbling his napkin.

"Chaos is having your whole world turn upside down

with the turn of a key." Another crawfish. Another tossed shell. Another glare.

"Chaos is not being able to pick your best friend out of a crowd of two." I leaned across the table. My eyes prickled, from sweat or spice or tears, I didn't know.

"Chaos is not knowing if your dad is alive or dead."

I suppose I did it to myself. Because as I said it, I *felt* him. Behind me. I turned, and there he was.

My dad.

He was grinning, his scruffy short whiskers shooting off his smile like fireworks in my heart. He had on his stained apron, the too-small one that said KISS THE COOK in strained letters across his barrel chest. He cocked his head at me.

"Jalen," he said. His voice! Low and commanding, like a big bass drum. I'd missed it so much. He took a step forward and picked up my hands. They looked small in his. They trembled.

"Jalen," he repeated. I nodded, speechless. I waited to hear how much he missed me, how much he loved me.

"You are no match for these Keepers. You will lose. You are just a kid."

I suppose I had known somewhere deep inside that it was a trick. Another nasty, spineless trick of Gemini's. But I wanted *so badly* for it to be real. I could pretend, too.

I threw my arms around his huge chest. They barely wrapped around his ribs, even now, four years later. I shook my head against him. "That's why I *will* win, Daddy. I have my whole future to fight for."

His body began to melt, to fade, to disappear. Again. I had been leaning on him, and I stumbled. My arms soon held nothing.

"No!" I screamed. I kicked Capricorn's cardboard box of shells. Crawdad skeletons and oyster shells fanned across the patio.

"Hey!" the other diners yelled, leaping to their feet. "Watch it!"

Capricorn collapsed, disappearing into rotten-egg mist, an unwelcome smell after all that food, after all that drama. Capricorn bleated his anger so loudly and fully, I felt a pang of envy that I couldn't do the same.

He rose from the mist in goat form, ducked his head under the table, and upturned it onto the couple next to us, covering them with greasy food and orange spices.

"Jalen," Brennan said. I looked at him in a daze. His eyes were urgent. "We need to go!"

Capricorn was already bobbing and weaving down Bourbon Street, bleating and ducking into the flock of tourists. We needed to catch him before he ran too far away.

I snapped awake like I'd been slapped. "Where did he go?"

I bumped and jostled through sweaty visitors, spilling drinks and food and apologies. This street was hotter than any other place we'd been today, it was so crammed with bodies. Plus, my shock was turning to anger. I was near boiling.

Purple and gold and green masks swooped between me and Capricorn like the ghosts of Mardi Gras past. Gold-spangled roadblocks, each masked tourist.

The food in my stomach rebelled. I swallowed bile. The Challenge hadn't been an eating Challenge, after all. That was just to slow me down, to make it almost impossible to catch Capricorn in a chase. And I had fallen for it. It *and* my dad.

"Jalen!" I managed a look over my shoulder before I rammed into the next sweaty, shirtless visitor. The agents. Running after us.

"Jalen, this isn't a game," Agent Cygnus yelled. *Tell me about it.*

Capricorn bleated a noisy *baaaa-aaa* and turned at the next block. Brennan and I followed. With two Ellies. I really despised one of those Ellies. I really did.

"Jalen, don't make us use force!" Agent Cygnus's voice carried to me around the corner.

The next block was bizarrely empty. Capricorn had left behind the bedlam of Bourbon Street for this quieter scene, a street filled with dusty antique stores.

Capricorn made a hasty turn onto Pirate's Alley, then slipped into a shallow doorway. The Ellies, Brennan, and I had him cornered.

But the agents had *us* cornered. Agent Griffin sprang forward and grabbed one of the Ellies. He whisked out his Maglite and put her in a chokehold, the metal flashlight tight against her throat.

Capricorn fainted, his bleat silenced. Brennan jumped on top of him.

Cygnus looked from the goat to the free Ellie to the Ellie trapped in his partner's chokehold. They could see it, all of it, ever since they'd held the book back on the bridge.

"Twins?" Griffin muttered, yanking the flashlight tighter against Ellie's neck. "Didn't see that in our notes."

"Yes, well," Cygnus sniffed. "If you won't cooperate with us, Jalen, we'll just take your friend here along with us. Until you give us what we want."

Ellie's eyes bulged above the Maglite that pressed against her windpipe, whether from fear or lack of oxygen, I didn't know. Her eyes changed color, behind her fear. The blue blackened, and Ellie's eyes grew dark as night.

I knew, then. They had Gemini. Gemini's twin, the one who had been my Ellie, my Nina, my mom, my daddy. The one I loathed.

I would win, wouldn't I, if I acknowledged who she was right now? I would beat Gemini at her own game at long last. The terror deepened in her black eyes. She knew that I had figured her out.

But I also knew that this Keeper *couldn't* end up in the

hands of these agents. No, that was far more dangerous than letting her masquerade as my family. What those agents would do with the kind of power Gemini possessed!

"What *do* you want?" I growled. Capricorn kicked and Brennan bucked, but he kept the goat under control.

"I already told you, Jalen," Agent Cygnus said, his voice as smooth as his slicked-back hair. "We want Ophiuchus's stone."

The trapped Ellie—Gemini's twin—made a gurgling sound. The other Ellie watched with horror, tears filling her blue eyes.

"I have the stone!" I said. "I already have it."

I reached down to my cargo pocket and tried to unfasten it. I hoped they didn't see my trembling fingers fumbling with the button. They'd know I was lying for sure.

"Here it is." I withdrew Virgo's cool, sleek sapphire. Its pure brilliance filled the doorway with soft blue light. I prayed the agents had no idea what Ophiuchus's stone might look like.

Agent Cygnus rubbed his palms together, licked his lips, and plucked the stone from my hands. He inspected it, then jerked his head at Griffin in a "turn her loose" command. Griffin threw fake Ellie to the ground. She landed in a wheezing pile of gasps. The other Ellie scrambled to help her.

The way Agent Cygnus looked at that stone, I knew for certain that he wasn't hunting Ophiuchus for the safety of all humankind, as he'd claimed. No, he wanted the power of the stone.

"You got what you're looking for," I said. My voice wavered. *Why* couldn't I lie well even now? "So leave us alone."

"Gladly," Griffin said. He pulled his partner's elbow toward the entry of the alley. "Gladly." Agent Cygnus couldn't take his eyes off the birthstone as he was led away.

I hoped Virgo would take it easy on me, after giving away her stone like that.

I hoped Virgo *wouldn't* take it easy on them.

And then all the food and the tragedy and the terror rushed up in a wave from my stomach. I vomited.

17

The Ellie on the ground dissolved into mist. Through the fog I could see her skin twist and morph. The messenger bag disappeared and transformed, becoming a tiny pouch, a draping toga. Blond ponytail lengthened into sleek black hair. A voice drifted through the fog.

It was Gemini in the fog. No, correction: It was Gemini's *twin*. Our original Gemini was now here, too.

"Jalen," the twin said. She stood and gripped my hand hard. "You bartered for my life, even though you knew I was a Keeper. You knew my birthstone couldn't end up in the custody of those agents, didn't you?"

I think I nodded. Gemini squeezed my hands harder. "You can be trusted not to abuse Ophiuchus's powers, yes?"

"Yes," I said, the sick taste lingering in my mouth. This was the mirror image of the Gemini who had guided us all this way. *This* being used her left hand instead of her right, her hair flowed to the opposite side, the folds of her toga wrapped to the reverse.

Gemini's twin turned to Ellie and laid a gentle hand on her shoulder. "I *think* I can trust Jalen. I *know* I can trust you. Make sure she finishes, okay?" She gave Ellie a quick hug. A tear slid down Ellie's cheek. She nodded and gulped.

Gemini's twin reached into the folds of her toga and withdrew a hefty agate, a solid stone swirled with orange and yellow. She handed it to me. I lifted it over my head and chanted, *"Sic itur ad astra."* Gemini floated into the heavens, and the light split, an identical pair of twinkling stars dancing home. It was beautiful, those twin lights spinning and twirling and completing each other.

Her voice was the last to leave us. It whispered in a trail behind her, "They'll hunt you until they win. Be wary."

Our guide, the Gemini left behind, watched and whispered, "Thank you, Castor and Pollux."

She then turned to us. "Jalen, *go!*" she urged.

Our feet pounded through Pirate's Alley. Brennan caught up to me, handing me Capricorn's birthstone. A blood-red garnet. I lifted it, still running, and panted, *"Sic itur ad astra."* Behind us, I sensed the lights lifting, felt Capricorn trot home.

Tears streamed down my face. The image of Ellie, crumpled on the sidewalk, had been seared into my brain. It wasn't my Ellie, of course, but for an instant, for the briefest of moments, I thought, *What if?*

What if they'd grabbed the other Ellie?

What if they'd captured Gemini's twin?

What if they get to Ophiuchus's stone before I do?

It was too much. I stopped. A sob escaped me.

"They wanted to hurt Ellie," I whispered.

Brennan nodded. "They know how to hurt you without hurting *you*."

"Not comforting."

Brennan laid a soft hand on my shoulder. "I know."

Ellie hunched beside me.

"Jalen, we have to go now," she ordered. "I made a promise. And Virgos always keep their promises. So move."

Brennan spit a laugh and hugged his sister. "She means it, Jalen. Let's go."

I smiled through my tears. And nodded. And kept going.

✳ ✳ ✳

Pirate's Alley bordered the gardens behind the Saint Louis Cathedral. The silvery triple spires of the cathedral scratched the early-evening sky like claws climbing into the heavens. The massive clock in the middle tower ticked away the seconds, taunting us before all of New Orleans. *Tick, tick, tick.*

It was 7 o'clock. We had an hour and a half until the sun moved out of the House of Ophiuchus, and two Keepers left to battle. Was it enough time?

"The Cathedral," Brennan huffed. "Let's hide in there until we can figure things out."

The square outside the Cathedral was swarming with tourists, but when we swung open the creaking, wooden doors and bounded inside, heaving and panting, it was silent. Every head in the church turned to look at the three dirty, loud kids who had just clattered in. Ellie turned pink, Brennan swallowed.

A wisp of incense burning in the corner somehow filled this gargantuan white space with the smell of spice. Then *tap, tap, tap.* Up the wide center aisle, striding across the black-and-white marble floor, was Virgo in her wedding dress. A bride leaving her ceremony.

She sauntered up to me and placed her bouquet on her hip, daisy petals sprinkling to the floor. I felt my heat rise. What would she do to me? I was really in for her wrath now.

But instead she placed a gentle hand on my shoulder. "I knew you'd be smart with that stone."

I blinked. "Did you get it back?"

Virgo smirked. "Of course I did."

Brennan cleared his throat. "The agents? . . ."

Virgo waved him off with a flip of her wrist. "Let's just say they'll be tied up for a while." Ellie grinned at her new horoscope Keeper.

"Did I win?" I asked Virgo. "The challenge with you, I mean."

She cocked her head like she didn't understand.

"When you left without your birthstone—" I started.

"I left the birthstone because I knew you'd need it," Virgo said. "That, and I could return to earth without being called by a Challenger if I left it behind. I owed you."

"But why?" I asked.

Virgo blinked. "You know why I think you granted me that kiss, Jalen?" she asked. I shook my head.

"Because you're young."

The fiery coal in my stomach flared. Again, with the youth.

"Don't look like that, Jalen," Virgo said. "I mean, you've never even been kissed, have you?"

The fire now blazed across my cheeks. Had she *really* asked that in front of Brennan?

"It's a compliment, Jalen. You still believe in true, pure love. And it exists, Jalen. It does. Adult humans forget that sometimes."

That I knew.

"But the young, they believe." Virgo leaned close, lightly pinching my chin. "You won because you know that true love *does* exist," she whispered. "And you know what else?"

I shook my head.

"Your father won, too."

I felt dizzy after sending Virgo to the heavens once again, this time with her birthstone. She hadn't answered any of my questions about my dad, and I didn't have time to press her. I couldn't stop picturing Dad, tangling with these creatures of the night. Had he won, overall? Maybe not. I needed to sit.

We slid into a pew, just behind a priest who was clutching a white string of rosary beads and murmuring softly.

"Father," Ellie whispered, tapping him on the shoulder. "Sorry to interrupt." Brennan and I exchanged a glance.

The priest startled, and his glasses flashed the red-yellow-orange of the stained glass windows as he turned. He scowled.

Ellie blinked. "I have a few questions. Please. It's important."

The priest's brow sank further. Ellie took his hesitation as an invitation to continue.

She swallowed. "Do you believe in astrology, Father? Horoscopes?"

The priest yanked his glasses off and pointed at us with the ear tips. "Absolutely not. And you better not be dabbling around in those evil arts, either, young lady. Nothing good can come of that."

Ellie nodded. She probably agreed with him on that point. The priest replaced his glasses and faced forward again.

"Father," Ellie continued, "what if there was no death? I mean, what if humans could somehow, well, *cure* it? solve the riddle? Reverse it? Wouldn't that be a good thing?"

The priest stood and bellowed. "Go, silly children with

your stupid questions! Go!" He shooed us with a wave of his wrist like we were pesky flies. His glasses flashed white, his eyes masked.

I grabbed Ellie's hand and pulled her toward the door. She started sniffling.

I thought of what the agents had told us, how millions of people around the globe were now unfit for their own lives. This priest was now one of them—that was clear. I cracked my knuckles.

"Don't be sad, Ellie," I whispered.

"I'm not *sad*, Jalen; I'm mad!" she snapped, swiping the tip of her nose. "Some people cry when they're mad." She looked up at the painted ceiling in an attempt to stop her angry tears. "All I wanted was an *answer*, you know?" Ellie blinked. "Something to let us know we're doing the right thing. A sign."

Brennan chuckled. "As in, *hey, babe! What's your sign?*"

I spit a giggle. Ellie's brow creased. Brennan and I held our breath, waiting for her to burst into tears or to yell at us. Old Ellie—the one I missed so terribly—would've totally cracked up at that.

Thankfully, she grinned through her tears. "Yeah. I guess we've had plenty of signs today, haven't we?"

I paused before we left Saint Louis Cathedral. Something about the mural on the ceiling made me look up, up, up until my neck hurt. The painting was full of oranges and yellows and reds; I probably wouldn't have been drawn to it before. It showed two distinct groups: one, a crowd of people on earth, worshipping together; the other, a crowd in the sky. That crowd was made up of angels and cherubs, with a golden bird in the center, radiating orange and yellow and red rays of hope.

What makes that priest so certain that astrology is evil? How does he know it so surely, when I still can't even say for certain what I believe, even after today? I mean, I still can't figure out what's *mine* to control and what belongs to Them, the crowd in the sky.

"I believe you can help us, ma'am." The voice was so clear, like a tiny crystal bell, it took me a moment to realize it wasn't one of the cherubs in the painting singing down just to me.

I spun around.

A small pair, apparently brother and sister, held hands behind me. They were identical to the cherubs in the mural above. Plump, rosy-cheeked. Blond corkscrew curls. Eyelashes for days, tears hanging like gems off the lashes of the little girl. I had to glance back up to the painting to double-check that the cherubs were still up there. They were.

"We need to find our home," the little boy said in a crisp British accent. "I believe you can help us?" His voice wavered at the end, betraying his fear.

I bit the inside of my cheek. Ellie, Brennan, and I had spent far too long in this cathedral already.

The little girl blinked. A diamond tear slid down her cheek. I couldn't leave them here. And leaving them with that priest didn't seem like a good idea; they were so scared already. I sighed and squatted beside them.

"Where are your parents?" I asked.

The boy shook his head, the girl's curls trembled.

"Okay," I said. "Let's look for them." I took each one by the hand. Brennan and Ellie followed. We led them around the Cathedral, whispering to groups of adults, "Excuse me, do you know where their parents are?"

One gruff guy looked at me, then at Brennan. "They're old enough to find their own parents."

The girl sobbed at that, and I kneeled to give her a hug.

"Two there!" came a voice.

I looked over the toddler's shoulder to see the man from the bus stop shuffling toward us, the one who'd helped us with food and clothes. Oh, what was his name? Being bad with names really stank.

"Henry!" Ellie said.

"Two there," Henry answered. "Two!"

I nodded. "Only one Ellie now. We're looking for these kids' parents. Can you help us?"

Henry shook his head violently. "No, no, no . . ."

"Okay, you don't have to help—"

"No kids. Fish."

That was all it took. The two children turned wavery,

watery, dissolving into mist. The gingham checks on their matching blue-and-green jumpers turned slick and slimy, morphing into gray, spotted skin. Golden ringlets of hair stiffened into fluttering gills, thickened into whiskery barbels. Wide pairs of eyes glassed over, bulged out, then slowly shifted to the sides of their heads. Their cheeks hollowed, flattened, drew forward. Their skin bubbled and gurgled, making sucking noises like rubber boots stuck in the mud. The duo collapsed on the floor of the cathedral and convulsed.

"Pisces," I said through the clearing mist. The pair of Louisiana catfish flopped and thrashed, agreeing with me.

Brennan wasted no time. He scooped up one of the huge, writhing catfish. "They were looking for their home. The river. Let's go!"

He turned toward the exit. I tried to pick up the other fish, the one that had once been a crying little girl. She writhed, bucking and hopping over the cathedral floor. Her catfish skin was slick, not scaly at all, and picking her up was like trying to pick up a twenty-pound glob of Vaseline. The other tourists in the cathedral were shooting me funny looks. That priest would be back here any second.

Finally, I wrestled the fish into a sideways position and carried it like a sack of potatoes. A strong, squirming sack of potatoes. The Mississippi River was near.

"You coming, Henry?" I asked the man.

"No, no, no!" Henry whipped his hair around, he shook his head so hard.

"Okay, Henry. Okay."

We hustled back through the massive wooden doors and into the twilight falling on Jackson Square, my arms aching from the strain. The statue of Andrew Jackson on horseback threw long shadows across the park.

Ellie caught up with me, breathless. "Sorry," she said. "I found the entry for Pisces." She ran next to me with the open copy of *The Keypers of the Zodiack* and huffed out the words.

> "*'Pisces, the fish. March 12–April 18. No soul places more trust in humanity than thou, dost Pisces. This allows for an intuition as deep as the seas, but leads to illogical, sentimental decisions. Thou art adaptable, however, so when thy self-pity crests—which it always does—swim deep in solitude and take comfort in thy heartfelt spirituality. Thou art perceptive, compassionate, and tolerant, which can make others cast their hooks at thee, seeking an easy catch. That which is easiest is not always best, Pisces.'*"

We ducked between art vendors, palm readers, and horse-drawn carriages to reach Decatur, the busy street between the cathedral and the river. Halfway across the intersection, the fish in my hands thrashed, slicing a deep gash across my left wrist with its gills, cutting me like a dull, jagged knife. I winced and dropped the fish. The catfish thumped to the ground. It flopped on the sun-warmed pavement, gasping for breath. I didn't have much time to get these fish home.

I bent to pick up the heavy, hopping fish, and heard a shrill screech followed by a horn blast. I looked up and saw my own reflection in the shiny chrome bumper of a taxi cab, inches from my face. I breathed a gasp and left a cloud on the chrome. "Move outta the way!" the driver yelled.

Picking up the bucking beast after it flailed on the dirty road was no easy task. Ellie grabbed the tail of the fish and motioned for me to get the head. Together, we carried the fish the rest of the way across the highway, over three sets of railroad tracks and toward the riverfront.

"No, no, no," Henry mumbled, scuffling up beside us.

"Henry, you don't have to come if you don't want to," Ellie said.

"No, no, no!"

Brennan was waiting for us at the riverside. The shore here was steep with jagged rocks. "I didn't know if we needed to toss them in together, or what," he said, still wrestling with his fish. We lined up beside each other on the river-bank. "On three," Brennan said, lifting his chin at the muddy water.

"No, no, no!" Henry grew more insistent.

"One," Brennan said. Ellie and I swung our fish backward. My stomach tightened suddenly. *That which is easiest is not always best.*

"Two." The increasing count made my pulse race. This wasn't right. Henry knew it. My gut knew it. And no one knows to trust instincts more than a Pisces.

"Three!"

"Wait!" I dropped my end of the fish and tackled Brennan and his fish. We tumbled and rolled across a few of those jagged rocks, a slick catfish squishing between us.

"Jalen!" Brennan said my name like a curse word. It felt like a knife.

"This isn't right." I hopped up and offered Brennan my hand. The fish flopped dangerously close to the wall of rocks leading down to the river. If it fell in from here, there would be no getting it back. Climbing down those rocks would be like climbing through a barbed-wire obstacle course.

"This—the river. This isn't their home," I said.

The fish Brennan had carried flopped two, then three more times. His body weight flumped down the rocky hill. I dived for the catfish, catching him by the slick tail. This fish was bigger than the other, weighing at least thirty pounds. Brennan, thankfully, caught *me* and dragged us both onto solid ground.

The catfish lay on the ground next to me. Both of us panted.

"Fish for fish," Henry said. He'd stopped me from throwing these fish in the river, thank goodness, but now he was telling me to fish for them? "Fish for fish." Henry gave me a thumbs-up, waggling his thumbs.

Ah, yes! It would be easier to *catch* this bottom sucker with a little noodling than try to pick him up again.

I stuck my thumb in front of his twitching whiskers and wriggled it, waiting for the pain. His jaw clamped down on my thumb like a wrench made of sandpaper. Once I felt the sting, I pulled with all my might and hugged the fish against my chest with my other arm. I stood with my catch. The catfish stopped thrashing and concentrated on trying to twist my thumb off.

"Whoa!" Brennan said with a half grin. "Where'd you learn how to noodle?"

I shrugged. "My dad was the best fisherman around." It felt good, remembering him like that, without a painful stab punctuating the end of the memory.

The other catfish, still laying on the riverbank, was no longer flopping. Its gills fluttered, trying to breathe. It gave a halfhearted flip of its tail fin.

"We have to go," I said. "We don't have much time." I carried the fish I caught with help from Henry.

Brennan picked up the dying fish, and Ellie grabbed its tail. "Which way?" he asked.

I looked around for the nearest, highest point. A point

that would give us enough height to send Pisces home. The spires of the cathedral, covered with silvery tiles that looked like fish scales, glinted.

"There," I said. "We have to go back."

We shuffled and hauled and scooted back across the railroad tracks, back across Decatur Street, back across Jackson Square.

The middle steeple of Saint Louis Cathedral held the clock. The smaller steeples had window-like openings on each side of their spires, I guessed for the bells. "There has to be a way to get up there," I said.

"There is," Brennan answered. We entered the narthex of the church again but turned immediately right, passing through a small, almost-hidden latticework doorway to a tight flight of spiral stairs.

"How did you know this was here?" Ellie huffed.

"Boy Scout trip," Brennan panted back.

I smiled. I could totally see After Brennan as a Boy Scout, but Before Brennan? Surprising.

My arms strained and my breath came in short puffs as we wound up and up and up the stairs to the top of the spire. The space grew smaller, tighter, hotter, and soon we could hear the clicking gears of the clock tower. Henry had to shuffle through the stairwell sideways. At last, we reached one of the shuttered window openings, and it swung open easily. I thought back to last night, when I'd leaned out of my own attic and unlocked Ophiuchus. When I'd had no instincts or gut reactions or beliefs whatsoever.

My thumb was raw and bloody from catfish teeth, but I managed to shove the huge fish through the small window. Brennan stood next to me, holding the other fish five stories above New Orleans.

"Do you think this is what Pisces meant?" Brennan asked. "About going home?"

I took a deep breath. "I hope so."

And then I let go. As I watched the fish plummet, I realized why people believe in things like heaven and astrology and higher powers. They believed in them because it was comforting to have order, to have a promise about the future, to categorize and make sense of our differences. They believed in them to feel connected—to the universe, to the cosmos, to each other—in some complex master plan. They believed because sometimes you just felt what was right and what was wrong, and there was simply no other way to explain any of it.

But the fish kept falling. I held my breath. Wasn't this what Pisces meant—going home? To the heavens? My instinct had told me to find a high spot, release them, and watch them fly home. But the fish kept falling.

And when the fish were inches, mere inches from the flagstone pavers so far below, a blue aquamarine birthstone thumped to the floor at my feet. I scooped up the stone and chanted, *"Sic itur ad astra."* The two fish illuminated and swam into the skies, swirling and twirling and twining into the heavens on their way home.

Believing doesn't mean having all the answers—just the opposite. *Believing* is having none of the answers and going forward anyway.

"Smart and strong, like her daddy," Henry said. "Like her daddy."

Then he turned and said again, earnestly, "Two there."

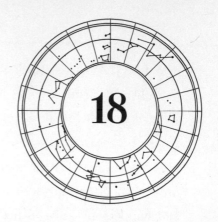

18

We said good-bye to Henry—he refused to come along any further, and I didn't blame him. I interpreted his mumbling to mean that he'd done this once before, with my dad. And he either didn't want to answer my questions, or he couldn't. So he gave each of us a smelly, gritty hug and pushed us on our way, telling us, "Two there," as a good-bye.

The black Lincoln slid down Decatur Street when we left Saint Louis Cathedral. We ran a few blocks west and hopped on the Saint Charles streetcar, which was thankfully at the stop. Ellie took deep breaths and closed her eyes, falling into a narrow wooden seat. Brennan and I each took a seat to ourselves, across the aisle from one another. The streetcar dinged its bell and moved forward, grumbling and jerking along steel tracks embedded in the streets of New Orleans.

My knees bounced and my eyes flittered from face to face, trying to decide which, if any, of our fellow passengers might be the last to attack and how. We had one battle left to fight: Aquarius. Would it be the driver, who hummed Zydeco tunes while he cranked the streetcar levers? Or the weary businessman, whose crooked necktie told of his already awful day? Or the mom bouncing the chubby toddler on her knee, or the toddler herself? Brennan reached over and cupped my knee in his hand. I suddenly remembered those scorpion stings, and how I hadn't felt them again until now. I cringed but nodded at Brennan. My knee stopped bouncing.

I leaned my head against the cool glass. It was about 7:30 p.m. We had one hour to go and one Keeper to meet. I prayed it was enough time. The streetcar clattered toward the Garden District, where the frilly Victorian homes looked like gingerbread houses trimmed in lace and icing.

My eyes were looking into the skies, up at the first stars melting into the early evening. There were more stars this evening than there were last night. That's why I didn't notice the water.

"Jalen!" Ellie breathed. She spun in her seat. "Look!"

Ellie had managed to keep her mind out of the clouds. She pointed to the sewer grates under the sidewalks; they were overflowing with water.

No, not just overflowing. They were spewing hundreds of gallons of water into the streets, over the roads and sidewalks and streetcar tracks. Panic rose, mixed with orange anger. New Orleans has a long history with rising water.

"The water bearer," Ellie said, fishing *The Keypers of the Zodiack* from her bag. "Aquarius."

> " 'Aquarius, the water bearer. February 16–March 11. To thou, Aquarius, uniqueness equates power. Thou art therefore highly focused on becoming as fresh and unpredictable as the rains. Be warned, however, that although thou strivest to be creative and visionary, many find thy originality to be moody rebelliousness, like that of a storm. And whilst thou takest pride in thy pursuits of the mind, thou oft forget the pursuits of the heart. This leads others to think of thee as chilly and impersonal. Thine insecurities art well-masked by thy strong, attractive personality. Because of this, thou art a master of deception.' "

I pressed my sweaty hands against the glass and stared at the water inching upward. Everyone else seemed oblivious to the water they were driving through in the streets, wading through on the sidewalks. Could it hurt them if they couldn't see it, couldn't feel it? I couldn't wait around to find out if Aquarius intended on harming all these people.

"We have to get off," I said. We pulled the wire overhead, the buzzer sounded, and the driver splashed to a halt in half a foot of rushing water.

"Have a great evening!" he sang. Brennan hesitantly hopped off the streetcar, over the current.

Ellie glared at the driver with knife-like eyes and jumped.

We landed with a splash near Lee Circle. We sloshed across the street and waded up the sidewalk. My panic level rose as the swirling, foaming water inched toward my knees, over a foot deep now, deep enough to sweep over small dogs. A nest of swamp rats burped out of a sewer grate, their orange eyes flashing as they tumbled by us on the current, hissing and cussing. The spring rains sometimes caused water to rise like this, and it was dangerous. My skin turned clammy.

"Who's doing this? Where's it coming from?" I asked, whipping about on the sidewalk, splashing and sloshing. I was high-stepping, trying to keep my balance in the never-ceasing rush of water. The floodwaters were dirty gray and smelled like sewage. Ellie held her messenger bag up near hunched shoulders, trying in vain to keep it dry. Brennan breathed in shallow pants. He was panicking in all this swirling, rising water. A nearby kid smirked and pointed at us, laughing with his friends. I could only imagine what we looked like to him, splashing and stepping through an invisible tide.

The water did nothing to douse my anger. "Aquarius!" I shouted over the roar of the blast. I hurled myself through water that now gushed over my knees. It took every bit of my effort, like walking against a river's current. "Don't be a coward! Show yourself!" The group of kids howled with laughter at that, and a few people on the sidewalk shuffled past me a little too quickly, giving me a little too much room when passing by. They hadn't handled the book; they couldn't see all this water that was causing my struggle.

A cackle drifted over the roar of rushing water. I spun and locked eyes with an old dark-haired woman peering out from beneath a red shawl. She hunched on a stool a few doors down, sitting outside a tiny restaurant. A wooden sign swung overhead, AGE OF AQUARIUS.

It was her! Aquarius stirred a pot of gumbo in a huge clay pot over an open flame. My eyes narrowed on her, her pot. Every time she stirred the pot, the water swelled.

My stomach gripped like a fist, watching her whip the waters around us. The water bearer, Aquarius, was *human*. Sure, all the signs had started out that way, but they'd changed into the forms of their constellations. The constellation Aquarius was a woman and her water pot. She wouldn't change.

I'd not battled a human yet, at least not directly. I'd fought animals of all shapes and sizes and numbers, and I'd had a hard enough time battling them. But Aquarius wouldn't morph into some gristly beast; no, she'd remain a woman. There was no way I could hurt a woman, even knowing she would rise to the skies. Seeing what could have been Ellie, choking and writhing in pain . . . no. I couldn't do it.

She flipped her wooden spoon in the thick stew, and the water swelled again. A wave splashed my chest. I scanned the area where we'd hopped off the streetcar; the water was almost to the nostrils of a child passing by in a stroller. I'd have to gather my gumption—*now*.

Brennan's panic finally got the best of him. He lunged at

Ellie, gripping her arm. Ellie's messenger bag slipped off her shoulder, splashed into the current, and was quickly swept down the street.

"The book!" Ellie yelled. She splashed down the street after her bag, but it was already far away.

I surged through the water, drenched, but it was like running in slow motion. The gumbo! Spill the gumbo, stop the flood. I dove toward the wrought-iron tripod holding the pot, and gallons of sausage and shrimp, rice and okra spewed out. The water in the streets disappeared instantly into thick mist and lifted like fog.

Aquarius bent over to right her tripod, her pot, over the still dancing flame. When she stood, her eyes were black as midnight. "You done mess wit da wrong sign, girl."

Aquarius ran her spoon in circles around the edge of the empty clay pot. Clouds churned in great gray circles, thunder rumbled across the sky. She *tinged* her spoon on the edge of the pot. A bolt of lightning sizzled from the clouds and struck nearby. Brennan jumped.

"Don' she wan' be with her daddy?" Aquarius asked, her black eyes locked on me. "Don' she wan' give in to see him again?"

Aquarius tossed her head back and laughed, whipping her spoon around inside the hollow pot. Rain pounded down, soaking us and everyone on the street, but the three of us were, apparently, the only ones who felt the chill of the downpour. Everyone else marched on, unaware.

It was so much rain, too much, and the streets began to fill with water again. But I just couldn't attack a Keeper in human form. Not after seeing Ellie's double crumple to the ground. It was too real for me. Had they discovered this was my weakness?

How would I stop this water bearer?

I felt a smile grow within me. The water *bearer*! A master of deception, Aquarius. The thing that bears water is the *pot*, not the woman!

I snatched a carved cane from the display at the shop next door. I reared the cane like a club and swung with all my might.

The large pot—a hollow clay pot, like so many I'd crafted with my own hands—cracked beneath my blow, fell to the sidewalk. The rain stopped like it had been turned off by a faucet. The pot shattered, but the fire beneath it remained strong.

Twelve Keepers, defeated.

I stood over the jagged shards of the broken pot and smiled.

I felt free.

I kicked aside the largest shard of the broken pot and found Aquarius's birthstone, a light purple amethyst. After my chant, the craggy old woman morphed into a youthful, flowing lady balancing a water jug on her head. She and her pot rained into the sky. I smiled, watching that pot take its place among the stars. Because there *was* a place for it.

Gemini placed her hand on my shoulders, like she had felt my soul change. "You should hurry," she whispered. "You need only to find Ophiuchus now."

I nodded and looked around for my friends. Ellie had chased her messenger bag for several blocks. The contents were strewn across the sidewalks. When we finally spotted *The Keypers of the Zodiack*, we saw it now rested under the toe of a pair of pointed black wingtip shoes.

Agent Cygnus stooped to pick up the ancient book. He tucked the book in his inside jacket pocket. When he looked up, his gaze landed on Gemini.

"It's you," he whispered. Agent Cygnus eyed Gemini the way a wolf eyes a sheep. If I didn't know better, I would've thought I saw fear flash across Gemini's face.

Agent Griffin approached us. "It's time you kids cooperate," he grumbled. He pulled back his jacket and showed us his leather holster. My stomach lurched.

"Didn't you know?" Ellie said. Behind her back, I could see her twist the handle of her messenger bag, knotting it in her fist. "We Virgos are known to be *uncooperative!*"

With that, she swung her messenger bag around, whapping Agent Griffin upside the head. Brennan lowered his shoulder and rammed Agent Cygnus with an *oof* to his gut.

Brennan upturned an empty café table with an open um-

brella in its middle toward the agents. The four of us—
Gemini beside us—ran toward the hospital.

"It's her! The one in the toga!" Agent Cygnus yelled. We
heard them scrambling over and around the wrought-iron
table.

The church bells chimed the quarter-hour.

8:15 p.m.

We had fifteen minutes.

19

Inside Touro Infirmary, we pounded up the steps, thinking that waiting for the elevator would surely put us in the claws of Agents Cygnus and Griffin.

"304," I huffed. Climbing three flights of stairs wouldn't normally be a problem, but there was nothing *normal* about this visit. "Room 304."

Just before we threw open the door to the third-floor hallway, Brennan grabbed my hand. I glared at him.

"Listen. I know we don't have much time, so just listen and don't fight me, feisty. I like you, Jalen, okay?" His face blushed bright red. "I mean, you know, as a friend? I always have liked you, and I always will. Once we turn back, we'll still be friends. I promise."

I looked from Brennan to Ellie, and my heart sank. The way this adventure had made our friendship grow was about to disappear. I squeezed his hand, then Ellie's. I'd miss them both. I'd even miss this version of Ellie, though with each second, I was closer to getting my best friend back.

"Sure," I choked out. I had to say it, or he'd keep insisting, taking more precious time.

We shoved into the hall, then threw open the door of Nina's room. "Nina!" I yelled. My voice echoed back to me.

The room was empty.

I felt my stomach rise into my throat. "Nina? Where are you? Ophiuchus?"

I searched the room for Nina, for Ophiuchus. Behind the partition. Under the hospital beds. In the bathroom. I was very familiar with every hiding place in these small rooms, from when I'd spent months here before. Where were they?

A nurse popped her head into Room 304. "What're you kids doing in here?"

I blinked, swallowed. "We're looking for my Nina. Uh, Asa Jones."

"Mrs. Jones?" The nurse's forehead loosened a notch. "Honey, she was discharged earlier today. Needs hospice care that one. We sent her home so family could say good-bye."

My ears started ringing so loud at the word "discharged," I hardly heard the rest. It was too much. Nina, so sick the hospital could no longer help her. Ophiuchus gone, too, apparently still with the one who needs healing. Us, fighting like warriors to get to her, all for nothing.

For nothing.

In ten minutes, earth would pass out of the House of Ophiuchus, and the world would be forever changed. My

Nina would no longer have the fighting chance she had before. My mom would be wandering the world in search of my dad. And I *still* had no answers about him. *Lost or left?* Who knew.

I turned to Gemini, my tears hot. "Where is she?" I growled. My heart ticked away our remaining seconds, the seconds until these personality changes were permanent. "Didn't I meet every Keeper? Didn't I win every Challenge?"

Gemini pulled out her metal nail file—*her nail file!*—and began sawing it over her fingertips. I snatched the file away from her and tried—unsuccessfully—to break it in half. Which added fuel to my fire.

"Didn't I win every Challenge?" I demanded.

Gemini cocked her head at me.

I counted through the Challenges in my head. Taurus, Cancer, Leo, Aries, Virgo, Libra, Scorpio, Sagittarius, Capricorn, Gemini . . .

Gemini.

The twins.

And suddenly it was as if all my fiery anger turned to candlelight, a gentle flame that helped me see. Gemini had ascended, then split into *two* persons, a pair. Our guide had whispered thank you to them both, to Castor and Pollux.

And Henry. He'd warned us over and over again. "Two there." He knew *both* Gemini twins were in one body, both morphing into Ellie and Nina and Mom and Dad. *Two there.*

This person who called herself Gemini—she would've been cast into the heavens alongside her stone, wouldn't she? *This* person was not a Gemini twin. Both twins were already accounted for.

"Gemini left with a warning. *They'll hunt you until they win,*" I repeated. *"Be wary."*

"But the warning wasn't for me," I said. "The agents aren't hunting me. They're hunting Ophiuchus. The warning was for you."

I swallowed. "You. You're her. You're Ophiuchus."

As I said it, this Keeper's skin melted like wax, then hardened, morphing from movie-star gorgeous into a stout, pudgy older woman with dimpled cheeks and a stooped back. She wore an old-timey nurse's uniform, flannel soft and white like a blanket, with a tiny hat and a skirt that swept the floor. A snake-and-staff pin gleamed over her heart, just like the one I wore. She smiled, no longer a brilliant, toothy spectacle, but a gentle smile, slow and sweet like warm honey.

It was her. Ophiuchus. The thirteenth sign.

"I don't understand," Ellie said. I startled at her voice; I'd forgotten anyone else was here. "You—Ophiuchus—you were with us the whole time?"

I shook my head. "But you told me that Ophiuchus would be with the one who needs healing."

Ophiuchus took my hands in hers. Her hands were warm and soft but strong. Comforting. Healer's hands. She smiled.

"I was."

✳ ✳ ✳

I'd been crafting hollow gray pots since my dad disappeared when I was nine years old. I'd thought I was fine. I see now that I'd needed a helping hand, but I hadn't known how to ask.

I had called Ophiuchus the Healer for me.

Ophiuchus withdrew her hands from mine, and I held her birthstone: a rainbow-colored topaz that changed colors when I moved. Ophiuchus's birthstone contained all the colors of the heavens. The stone that heals. All our wounds that we'd collected on this journey—the cuts, the stings, the bruises— had healed, all but disappeared. We hadn't even noticed.

I held so much power in my hands right now. This stone could heal my Nina. Did I have to send Ophiuchus to the skies? Couldn't I keep her here, save my Nina? Wouldn't the rest of the world eventually adjust?

"Jalen." Brennan shifted his weight and pointed at the clock over the door. 8:28 p.m. Tears streamed down Ellie's cheeks. "Do it, Jalen," she whispered.

All I had to do was lift the topaz stone over my head and chant. Could I do it? Did I *want* to?

Brennan nodded at me, encouraging me to go ahead, say it. Brennan. Would he and I still be friends, as he had promised? I doubted it. I hadn't realized how much I'd missed his friendship these last few years. I would surely miss it again if I cast Ophiuchus to the skies.

And Ellie. She had saved me so many times, on so many levels today. I'd never see this Ellie again. I'd miss her like part of *me* was missing.

8:29 p.m.

And me.

Will I still be able to ask for help when I need it?

Will I still have the fire?

Will I be happy?

Footsteps echoed in the hall. The agents!

Ophiuchus hugged me. "Just know that if you use it," she whispered, "one life is substituted for another."

I felt like I'd been bitten by a snake. I managed to lift my hands and shout, *"Sic itur ad astra!"*

And then I blacked out.

✳ ✳ ✳

I heard the buzzing of the fluorescent lights in the hospital room. A pinprick of blue-green light flickered, then my vision slowly opened.

"Jalen?" a voice said with a tinge of panic. "C'mon, Jalen. Wake up."

"Mom?" I said. "Nina?" My vision returned. Ellie, Brennan, Agent Cygnus, and Agent Griffin huddled over me.

Ellie sighed with relief, then giggled. "I'm not quite *that* old, Jalen."

I smiled. She was back. I started to sit up, but my stomach lurched.

"No, lay back down," whispered Agent Griffin. "You took a nasty spill. I'll go get the nurse." He patted my shoulder and tiptoed away. This, the same agent who had threatened my best friend.

Agent Cygnus whipped around and kicked the wall. He leaned over me and flashed the spine of *The Keypers of the Zodiack* at me, still tucked in his jacket pocket.

He whispered with peppermint-chilled breath, "We'll figure out how to unlock it. And when we do, we'll get that birthstone from Ophiuchus."

He shoved me—hard—with the pointy toe of his wingtip shoes, then stormed away. Ice ran through me. I realized suddenly that my fingers were twining in a lock of my hair. I pulled a strand across my face. Hot pink.

I lay there on the floor of the hospital room, listening to Ellie and the nurse who'd scuttled in exchange knock-knock jokes in what I guess was an attempt to lighten the mood. The nurse shined a tiny flashlight in my pupils. "You're going to be fine," she said at last. I hoped she was right.

"I think I'm okay," I said.

Brennan chuckled and slumped in the only chair in the hospital room. The nurse left to get me some water. After a few moments, I felt like I could sit. I pulled myself up on my elbows, and a clunk sounded. A thud, falling out of my open cargo-pants pocket.

On the floor. Ophiuchus's birthstone.

She'd left it behind, hidden it with me. What did this

mean? When Virgo left her stone behind, she'd been able to return without being called. Would Ophiuchus return? And the power! Could I heal Nina?

Why do I still have this stone?

I picked it up and felt a familiar spark. Not a too-brilliant spark, sharp and fiery, but a slow, solidifying warmth. The heat that completes the pot.

This stone had healed me *twice*.

My dad *had* won. He had held this very stone in his hands, and Ophiuchus had given him the same instructions. "If you use it, one life is substituted for another."

He'd used the stone to heal me when I was nine and so sick I was supposed to die. The doctors had told him they'd tried everything, that they'd exhausted every resource. So he did the only thing he could think to do: He turned to Nina and Madame Beausoleil. He had left intentionally, and he had lost his life.

He'd given up his life for me. Left *and* lost. No absolutes.

20

"Nina?" I whispered into the darkness. A wedge of light from the hallway sliced into her bedroom. She stirred under the sheets, and it took my breath away. The last time I had seen her, Nina had still been a woman of curves and cushion. She was now a woman of angles and edges.

"Jalen?" she whispered through cracked lips. "You did it. You found Ophiuchus."

"You knew?"

She nodded, her thin hair fanning across her pillow. "I've changed that way once before." She tried to smile. It looked like it took every bit of her effort.

Ophiuchus's stone burned against my leg. I could use it right now. I could save her. I *should* save her. Shouldn't I? The world could use more Ninas.

She patted the bed, and I curled up next to her. The stone in my pocket felt like it was pulsing. Nina put her arm over me. It felt dry and thin, like a twig.

"It's my time, Jalen," she whispered into my hair. I realized my cheeks were wet. "Let's do this with dignity."

I nodded. I couldn't save Nina. As much as I wanted to save her, replacing Nina's life with another was not an option. Another death, even one somewhere far off in the world, would ripple through the order of the universe, like wedging a thirteenth sign into the zodiac calendar. I couldn't give some other girl in some other family a white shock of hair just to keep my Nina here with me.

Losing Nina felt like watching a brilliant, shooting star streak across the sky: The beauty wasn't here long enough. But I ignored the stone that practically throbbed in my pocket and instead unfastened the snake-and-staff pin over my heart.

I pinned it onto Nina's nightgown with shaking hands. "With dignity."

The next evening, the bells on the door of Madame Beausoleil's shop dinged. My mom poked her head in the door, between the rows of alligator teeth. It was odd seeing her here. She was too solid for a place like this, like a human walking among ghosts. She never used to come here with Daddy, once upon a time.

"Jalen, honey, we need to go," she said. "It's been exactly one hour. I don't want to stay away from Nina for long." She was right. I didn't want to leave Nina alone for too long, either. I wanted to spend every minute I could with her, while I still could. But I had to make sure we'd be safe.

Ellie pleaded, palms pressed together, in overly dramatic fashion. "One more minute, *please*, Mrs. Jones?"

My mother's forehead wrinkled. She looked at her watch but nodded. "Ellie Broussard, you are a bad influence on my daughter." It was as close to a joke as my mom was capable of telling, and if you didn't know better, it came out sounding like an insult. Two days ago, I would've thought it was one.

But Ellie knew, had *always* known, about my mom. She laughed as the door closed. "Hurry, Jalen. That's as much time as I could buy you. Oooo that stupid Brennan, bailing on us."

Yes, it likely would've been easier to stay if Brennan had driven us. But he'd canceled on us because he was auditioning to drum in a new band. He'd muttered that it "far outweighed toting around a couple of middle school kids." I hoped he got the gig, though I wasn't sure he'd invite us to any of his shows. It was silly to even think it, but changing Brennan back felt like watching a favorite earring roll around the sink and slip down the drain. One was still left, but what can be done with it?

Madame Beausoleil perched on her stool behind the counter. "So you'll keep the lock safe?" I asked her.

She nodded slowly. "Guess you *were* ready."

I shrugged. "They have the book." I shuddered at the

thought of it. All that power, all those words that could shape the future. But as long as we kept the lock and the key away from them, we were safe. I hoped.

"I figured dat."

"And Nina's wearing the pin. I think it's giving her some fight back." I knew as I said it that it wasn't true, but Nina would want Madame Beausoleil to think that. That she was exiting with her chin held high. With dignity.

"Good. De old gal need it."

The dusty store fell silent for a moment. "What you gonna do with de stone, girl?" Madame asked.

I blinked. I hadn't said a word about Ophiuchus's stone. I patted it now protectively. Ellie had given me her messenger bag, and I kept the stone with me at all times. I didn't trust it to be anywhere away from me. But honestly, I didn't trust it with me, either. My fingers flew to my lock of hair, dyed purple now, and started twisting.

My voice dropped to a whisper. "Do you want to see it?"

Madame Beausoleil almost slipped off her stool, she shook her head so violently. "No. Nuh-uh. I dint wan see it when her daddy brung it in here, and I don wan see it now."

I looked at the dirty floor of her shop and smiled. "Nina brought him here for the book, didn't she? When I was sick. Before."

Madame Beausoleil nodded. "I wouldn't give dat book to jest anyone. Your daddy, he begged. He returned it, too, jest before he——" Her words dropped off. She was unsure of what to say around me.

"Died," I finished. I swallowed, but nodded. "But how come no one told me about this? How come *Nina* never told me?"

Madame Beausoleil's cloudy eyes softened. "You tink your Nina wan you to live wit da guilt of knowing your daddy give his life for yours? Dat's not something you tell a child."

It *wasn't* something you tell a child. But I knew it now.

"I don't know what I'm going to do with the stone," I admitted at last. I had so many questions: Why did I have this thing? Did Ophiuchus think I needed it? Was Ophiuchus planning to return? Did she *want* me to heal Nina? "I'm kind of scared I might do something stupid with it."

Madame Beausoleil chuckled, and it sounded like she had gravel in her lungs. "Nah, girl, you a Sagittarius. Dey think before making dey choices. Dat's always good, right?" She spun on her stool, waddled off of it, and shuffled behind the curtains into the back.

I grinned. Because, well——not always. Sometimes thinking too much could make you miss something really great. Come to think of it, I don't know that there is such a thing as a *good* trait or a *bad* trait. Every aspect of our personalities can be good or bad; it just depends on the situation. Sometimes a help, sometimes a hindrance. No absolutes.

Take my dad, for instance. He was stubborn. And naive. And obsessive. But he *had* to be those things to defeat all twelve Keepers. He was also curious and patient and loyal and faithful. Faithful, I think, most of all. Daddy needed all those traits to win. No absolutes.

I smiled. It felt good, remembering him without the stabbing pain. Remembering the joy and happiness and love instead. It would be how I would remember Nina, too. With dignity.

The sounds of New Orleans drifted in through the front door: a delivery truck splashing through a puddle, a tourist asking for directions, the *sizzle-pop-psst* of a street vendor frying up something spicy on a street corner. And underneath and over it all, a line of jazz, with its deep-blue blurts and snappy-red blasts and twists and turns and twirls. Life moving forward. No absolutes.

I caught myself twining my fingers in the purple streak in my hair. The salt-and-pepper snake in the glass box on the counter looked at me, then. It cocked its tiny diamond head and winked.

And I winked back.

Traditional 12-Sign Zodiac

Aries: March 21–April 19

Taurus: April 20–May 20

Gemini: May 21–June 20

Cancer: June 21–July 22

Leo: July 23–August 22

Virgo: August 23–September 22

Libra: September 23–October 22

Scorpio: October 23–November 21

Sagittarius: November 22–December 21

Capricorn: December 22–January 19

Aquarius: January 20–February 18

Pisces: February 19–March 20

The 13-Sign Zodiac

Aries: April 19–May 13

Taurus: May 14–June 19

Gemini: June 20–July 20

Cancer: July 21–August 9

Leo: August 10–September 15

Virgo: September 16–October 30

Libra: October 31–November 22

Scorpio: *November 23—November 29*
Ophiuchus: *November 30—December 17*
Sagittarius: *December 18—January 18*
Capricorn: *January 19—February 15*
Aquarius: *February 16—March 11*
Pisces: *March 12—April 18*

Thank you for reading this FEIWEL AND FRIENDS book.
The Friends who made

The 13th Sign

possible are:

Jean Feiwel, publisher

Liz Szabla, editor-in-chief

Rich Deas, creative director

Elizabeth Fithian, marketing director

Holly West, assistant to the publisher

Dave Barrett, managing editor

Lauren A. Burniac, associate editor

Nicole Liebowitz Moulaison, production manager

Ksenia Winnicki, publishing associate

Anna Roberto, assistant editor

FIND OUT MORE ABOUT OUR AUTHORS AND ARTISTS
AND OUR FUTURE PUBLISHING AT
MACKIDS.COM.

OUR BOOKS ARE FRIENDS FOR LIFE